Also by D.M. Chappell

<u>Matchmaking Series:</u>

The Truth About Fairy Tales (Matchmaking Agency)

<u>Medallion Series:</u>

The Liberator's Medallion

Ersha's Revenge

The Truth About Prince Charming

By D.M. CHAPPELL

Copyright © 2019 by D.M. Chappell

Cover Design: The Book Design House

Cover Shadow Art Graphics: Dahn Tran Art

Library of Congress Control Number: 2019900008

ISBN: 978-0-9981183-6-9

This book is a work of fiction. Names, characters, places, and incidents are the products of the author's imagination or are used fictitiously. Any resemblance to actual events, locales, or persons, living or dead, is entirely coincidental.

Printed in the U.S.A.

ACKNOWLEDGEMENTS

Thank you to my crew: Jason, Belinda, Shelly, and Amy for their assistance with this most recent project. I couldn't have done it without you! And of course, thanks to my wonderful husband, Eric, who continues to support my obsessive need to write.

The Truth About Prince Charming

Chapter One

False positive. Those were two words I would add to my most hated list. I'd put them right behind unfaithful, divorced, and PCOS (Polycystic Ovary Syndrome). At first, I wasn't certain how I'd felt about seeing the two pink lines on the test, besides being numb and utterly stunned.

After trying unsuccessfully for over a decade with my ex-husband, Mike, to bear children, I hadn't believed I *could* get pregnant. That was also why my current live-in boyfriend—and detective—Jack and I hadn't ever broached the subject. It had been a shocking discovery for us both. But together we'd come to terms with it, and I'd let a spark of excitement ignite in my soul.

It wasn't as if I'd only taken *one* test and believed what

it showed me was true. I had taken three different tests, all with the same result. Now, as I occupied the seat across from my doctor and listened to her explain to me how PCOS could oftentimes deliver a cruel false positive, I felt the spark die to nothingness.

A gentle squeeze of my hand from Jack—who was positioned on the chair beside me—brought my attention back to the current conversation.

"Are there any other questions, Ms. Bloom?" Dr. Imperial asked me, her tone soft.

"No. Thank you for the explanation. I should've known better than to get excited."

She reached over and patted my hand, a gentle smile on her face. "Now, now, Ms. Bloom. You can't think like that; miracles happen every day."

I smiled, but I knew it looked as fake as it felt—and as it actually was. I was too emotionally drained to pretend.

As far as miracles went, I didn't expect any more of those to come my way anytime soon, if ever again. In the last year I'd had two miracles happen: a bullet—fired at me by an ex-T.A.F.T. employee—had missed by mere inches thanks to a bit of help from Jack. And, I'd found my one true love, again with help from Jack. I guessed I could perceive it as Jack being the miracle, since he was involved with both events. In either case, a girl couldn't expect lightning to strike a third time.

"Thanks for your time," Jack said, as we stood. He reached out his hand to the doctor. "We appreciate the information."

Dr. Imperial shook his hand. "I wish I had better news for you, but don't give up hope. If you still want to pursue this path, we can put together a game plan."

I maneuvered my way to the door, feeling claustrophobic and wanting nothing more than to just leave. "This isn't a road we were intentionally trying to traverse, given our ages. We were just willing to accept that it had happened. However, we'll let you know if we change our minds."

Dr. Imperial nodded but remained silent as Jack quickened his pace and followed me outside to the checkout desk. Once we were all squared away, we headed out to the car.

After we were situated, Jack began to press the engine start button but stopped. "Are you sure you're okay?"

"Yes and no." I slumped in my seat and let my head fall back against the headrest. "Not having kids is something I'm okay with. But, that doesn't mean I'm not disappointed. The thought of having *your* baby made me happy."

"Me too." Jack reached over and squeezed my hand for just a moment before returning it to the wheel. "Do you have any interest in trying again?"

"Not really. If it happens by itself I'm fine with it, but I don't want to purposefully try. If you feel differently though, we can discuss it."

"No need to discuss; I'm fine with your plan." Jack

exhaled and I could feel the release of tension in the air. Clearly, he'd been worried about where I stood. I was glad to know my answer matched his own.

As I reflected on the whole topic, I remembered something ... the baby outfit. I blinked back tears as I pictured the tiny onesie that sat in my top dresser drawer. I hadn't intended to buy anything for the baby-to-be when I'd gone to the mall to pick up some other items, but when I had seen it in the storefront window it called to me. It was a creamy, pale yellow with a multi-pastel-colored elephant on the front. Tiny pearl snaps ran the length of the outfit. Not knowing whether our future child would be a girl or boy, the neutral-sex color had seemed appropriate.

Lowering my hand to my stomach I massaged out the invisible knot I felt deep inside at the idea of having to give the item away. I knew keeping the item would be a bad move; it would only remind me of the loss. As I added the task to my to-do list, another thought floated through my mind. At that thought I tilted my head to peer at Jack, a thin smile on my face. "At least we can focus on the bright side."

"Yeah? What's that?"

"Because we didn't tell anyone our news, no one else has to survive a broken heart today."

Jack let out a quivering exhale. "I guess that is a bright side. So, now what?"

"Now, we enjoy being normal and boring. I'm positive we've had more than enough excitement lately to last a lifetime."

"Normal and boring sounds good to me. I mean really, what else could go wrong?"

Chapter Two

Later that evening we pulled into my father's driveway. It had become a weekly ritual to join Dad and Grandma for dinner on Friday nights. I'd gotten lucky that both of them had welcomed Jack with open arms. The fact that Jack had saved my life probably had something to do with it, though.

"Hey there, kiddo," Dad said, as we walked onto the front porch where he was sitting and rocking in his chair.

I noticed the front yard and porch of my parents' house was once again in tip-top shape. A few months ago the large, two-story, buttercream Victorian with white shutters had been a tiny bit worse for the wear. Neither Dad nor Grandma had been in any shape to take care of the large house.

Jack—being the sweetheart that he was—had stepped in and helped out. He'd been careful to do it slowly, so what he was doing wasn't obvious. He hadn't wanted to rub Dad the wrong way by working to spruce things up. However, had it not been for Jack, I would've hired someone. I knew Dad would never consider moving, so that idea was off the table, but that didn't mean I couldn't help out to keep the house up.

"Hey, Dad," I replied, as I bent down to kiss him on the cheek. "Where's Grandma?"

"In the kitchen," he said. "Dinner should be about ready."

He stood and followed Jack and me into the house and towards the kitchen. The earthy aroma of pot roast and all the fixins' wafted through the house. My stomach let out a rumble of hunger.

As Dad had foretold, Grandma was in the kitchen setting the table. Even though the table was a bit tight for four people—when there was as much food as Grandma was known for fixing—it was extremely rare we ever used the formal dining room to eat, even when we were eating a meal because of a holiday or fancy occasion.

The dining room had always been mom's favorite room to eat in. She yearned for any occasion to pull out the good china and decorate it. We had tried once or twice to eat there after mom died, but whenever we did it just felt wrong somehow.

"Well hello, you two!" Grandma said when she stopped running around long enough to notice us coming in.

"Hello, Olive." Jack moved over and gave Grandma a kiss on her cheek. Grandma blushed as she always did.

Jack inhaled deeply. "It smells wonderful in here."

"Ditto," I concurred, my muscles relaxing as the scent of home wrapped itself around me.

"Is dinner almost ready?" Dad fidgeted in the doorway. "I'm starving."

Grandma—who was passing Dad at the moment he posed his question—reached out and jabbed him in the stomach. "I'm pretty sure you can wait a few minutes."

Jack hid his chuckle with a cough as he made his way to his designated seat at the table. Dad followed suit, pouting as he did.

"What can I help you with, Grandma?" I asked.

Grandma pointed at the fridge. "Just grab the butter, Flower."

Grandma was the only living individual who was allowed to call me by that nickname. I'd been cursed with the full name of Calla Lily Bloom. My mother had thought it sounded lovely; I did not. It was hard enough to make it through childhood with a regular name, much less with one like mine. Jack had called me "Flower" once; it didn't end well for him.

I walked over to the fridge, grabbed the butter, and took it to the table. I plopped down into my own seat as

Grandma placed the final item—the roast—on the table and took a seat. We gave a quick blessing, then dug into the food.

It didn't take long at all for second helpings to be served to the boys and all of our plates to be emptied. When I saw the look of disappointment on Jack's face when he looked at all the empty dishes, I was surprised he didn't lift his plate to his face and lick it clean just to have one more taste. He sure did love Grandma's cooking.

"You've outdone yourself again, Olive!" Jack wiped his mouth with his napkin and leaned back.

"No need for flattery, Jack. You've already got my granddaughter's affections." Grandma grinned and stood to clear the table. I shooed her down.

"You sit, Grandma. I've got the dishes. You did all the cooking!" I took the dish out of her hands and moved around the table to pick up the rest of the empty dishes.

Grandma sank back down without any argument. That's when I knew something wasn't quite right.

"You feeling okay?" I stopped in place and eyed her carefully.

Grandma waved me away. "Stop your worrying, child. I'm fine. The ole' bones just aren't what they used to be."

I glimpsed at Dad to see if he had anything to add; he just shrugged. This either meant he had nothing to add, or he'd already tried to pry the information from her earlier.

"Now you two knock it off. I told you I'm fine. That's the end of it." She split her gaze back and forth between the two of us for a moment before turning and firmly planting it on Jack. "Besides, we have much more interesting things to talk about."

Jack's face blanked. "We do?"

Grandma let out a huff and balked. "Being a fancy detective and all, you've got to be part of the police blackvine, acquiring all the juicy details on the lady killer thought to be coming our way."

The "blackvine," as Grandma called it, was like the grapevine, but for all the super-secret gossip. Her particular vine was how we received a fair amount of our intel on prospective selection pool candidates—the men who made up the pool our clients picked from.

Jack grimaced. "Oh, I see where you're going. Sorry, Olive. You know I can't give out specifics on ongoing investigations."

An ornery grin spread across Grandma's face and she wiggled her eyebrows up and down. "Not even for some fresh strawberry-rhubarb pie with homemade vanilla ice cream?"

When Jack remained silent, Grandma added, "I even used one of those fancy whole vanilla beans, just like you like it."

Grandma knew how much Jack like vanilla ice cream with real vanilla bean added, and she wasn't above bribery.

Jack wet his lips. "You're killing me, Olive. You know I can't tell you, no matter what you butter me up with."

"That's too bad," Dad chimed in, a big smile

spreading across his face. "More for me then!"

"Dad," I chided from the sink where I was rinsing off the dishes. "Be nice."

Grandma—being her sweet self—meandered over to the counter, sliced a large piece of pie, added a huge scoop of ice cream, and then sauntered back to the table where she waved the pie under Jack's nose before setting it down at her spot. I swore a tear almost rolled down Jack's cheek.

"Oh, for crying out loud." I stomped over to the table, grabbed the plate, set it down in front of Jack, and handed him a spoon. Without hesitation, Jack grabbed the spoon, mouthed "I love you," and dug in.

"Hey, wait a minute—" Grandma started.

"Leave the poor man alone," I reprimanded. "I'll tell you what I know. We'll see how long he lasts before he corrects me on anything I inaccurately state."

I learned early on that Jack had two flaws: he couldn't let people tell a story without cutting them off, and he couldn't stand when misinformation was circulated.

Jack shook his head and grunted, but didn't stop or put his spoon down. Had his hands not been full, he would've been pinching the bridge of his nose with his fingers. A telltale sign he was doing his best to hold in his aggravation.

I smiled sweetly, served the rest of us pie and ice cream, and then slid into my chair. "What I heard is that the 'guy' has hit all the surrounding towns. He takes a woman for all her money, then murders her."

Jack didn't correct or interrupt me, so it appeared I had stated it pretty close to the truth.

"Sounds like those other counties' detectives must be a bunch of half-witted idiots. You'd reckon they could connect the dots and figure out who the guy is. It's not like women can keep any secrets when it comes to dating or men for that matter." Dad made sure to stare squarely at Grandma when he made his declaration.

Grandma puffed out her chest, not from indignation but from pride. She took immense satisfaction from her status as a gossip legend. "You've got that right, George. I mean, how hard could it be to catch a guy like that? Just match up the pictures the ladies took. Voila, you unveil your killer."

"It's not that easy, Olive," Jack interjected, now done devouring his dessert. "The guy keeps changing his persona each time, never lets anyone snap his picture, and he never picks the same type of woman twice."

I smirked, knowing that Jack had been fighting a losing battle in holding back information. The only reason he hadn't jumped in sooner was because his mouth had been full. "What about the victim's friends; surely they've got a description?"

"The friends all say they never met the man in person, and the verbal descriptions the victims gave were all different. One told her friends he had brown hair, blue-eyes. The next said he was blonde with green eyes. The only constant is his rough height and build."

"So, you don't have any suspects at all?" Dad asked.

"Not so far. The only thing found to date is an unidentified partial print, and a possible clue on where he might be headed."

"I'm guessing that would be Belmont, since you're involved?" Grandma asked.

"Perceptive as always." Jack smirked. "The Waynesville police department found both a Google search for Belmont on the most recent victim's laptop and a few receipts scattered over the last few months for Junior's Restaurant on Birch Street."

I tilted my head. "Is that why you think he's either here or coming this way, because of Google and a few receipts?"

"It's thin, I know." Jack shrugged. "But it's the only lead we have at this point. We're hoping if we do a group task force and combine our evidence and manpower, we might be able to catch him before he strikes again. And, if he's in Belmont, the bastard is mine."

"Sounds to me like you should be letting T.A.F.T. help you. We've got the best matching algorithm in the state. You might not be able to get a description of him or figure out who he might target, but we could," I mumbled in between bites of food.

Jack snapped upright in his chair. "That just might work!"

I stopped my fork halfway to my mouth. "You're not serious. I was only joking."

"Why wouldn't it work?" Grandma asked. "All we

need to do is plug in the details of all the women we know he dated and killed. It should calculate out what things they *did* have in common if it's not based on appearance."

I lowered my fork, leaned back, and thought about it. *I guess it could work ...*

A wide grin spread across Jack's face. "I've got all the reports from the different stations; we could start plugging them in tomorrow."

Not only did Jack love catching bad guys, he loved solving puzzles. Thank God for that, or I wouldn't still be here today.

"Well, I don't suppose it could hurt to give it a try." I shrugged, still contemplating the possible percentage of success.

"Can I help? I want to be deputized too!" Grandma's eyes sparkled.

"Oh, dear Lord!" Dad—speaking to no one in particular—lowered his head into his hands.

Jack tried to hold in a laugh but failed. "Sorry, Olive. We wouldn't deputize anyone, but you might have to fill out a confidentiality form. I'll need to ask the Captain."

"Good, it's settled then. What time do you want me to come over?" Grandma asked.

Heaven help us all!

Chapter Three

We had barely gotten out of bed before Grandma was at our door the next morning. Lucky for her, she'd come bearing gifts: breakfast sandwiches and coffee from Where You Bean.

Grandma had her normal Kitchen Sink—equivalent to a Trenta at Starbucks—sugar-free caramel, triple shot espresso, with fat-free milk. For me, she delivered a Gimme More: no water, extra spice chai latte, almond milk, with extra foam. And last but not least, a Big Boy: straight-up black coffee for Jack. Since none of us were morning people or good on an empty stomach, it was a smart move on her part.

She laid the bounty down on the counter in my office

as we got situated. Jack and I had stopped at the police station on the way home the night before and picked up all the boxes of notes on the previous crime scenes. They were now scattered around my office floor.

I loaded T.A.F.T.'s algorithm program onto the computer and then moved out of the way so Jack could man the computer.

"Jack, why don't you build a profile for each of the victims. Just type in the basic data from your intake forms and fill in as many lines as you can." I slid the first file folder toward Jack. "Grandma, go ahead and start reviewing the witness statements and try to help fill in the missing blanks. I'll peek at the crime scene photos and see if I can figure out any of the ladies' preferences based on their apartments, clothing, etc."

Jack turned his gaze to me, his lips pressing into a fine line. "Are you sure you want to review them? It's not easy to unsee death once it stares you in the face."

"I'm a big girl. I can handle it," I snapped.

Jack held up his hands in surrender and returned his attention back to the computer. I didn't mean to snap at him—he was just trying to protect me—but nothing rubbed me wrong quicker than a man telling me I couldn't/shouldn't do something because it might tarnish my delicate sensibilities.

I took a deep breath and opened my first folder. The angle made it appear as if it were staged for one of the crime TV shows everyone was watching these days. I tried to keep distance in my mind between the picture and reality. The less real I made the image, the less likely it was to haunt me later. It was clear, however, no matter how I analyzed it, this victim had died from multiple gunshot wounds to the chest.

After doing a swift inventory of what the woman had on, I concentrated on viewing the apartment itself, rather than the dead body on the ground. Jack's police files should've had all the physical description details, so I didn't feel it necessary to spend the emotional power on those items. I jotted down all the particulars I thought might be beneficial to the profile.

By the time the three of us had performed our duties, the first profile was eighty-five percent complete, and we had all finished off our libations.

"Do you believe this amount of data will produce results for us once we get all four women's profiles built?" Jack asked.

"It should get us pretty close. Though it would be nice to obtain a smidge extra ... " My words drifted off as I contemplated how we could get more.

"I'll tell you what"—Grandma crossed her arms over her chest—"If you two tell me what's going on with you, I'll call in a few favors and get those blanks filled in."

"Favors?" I asked at the same time Jack repeated, "What's going on?"

We both had the same confused expressions on our faces.

"Yes, favors. I can get some of my friends to help me dig up more people we can speak with who knew the victims: classmates, roommates, workmates. All the people the dim-wits at the other stations didn't bother to follow-up with."

Jack reached up and pinched the bridge of his nose but bit his tongue. He'd learned it best not to look a gift horse in the mouth, especially when that horse was Grandma.

When it was clear neither of us was going to say anything about her topic, Grandma continued. "I know you two are hiding something major. You've both been stressed out for the last week, and last night you both looked awful. So, spit it out."

I should have known. Grandma always had a Spidey sense when it came to knowing when someone close to her was hurting. Jack and I gazed at each other, and I shrugged, knowing Grandma wasn't going to stop until we told her what she wanted to know.

"How about we go in the other room, take a break, and we'll fill you in?" I said.

She agreed, so we all moved into the other room. It was going to be rough to break the tragic news about the loss of the great-grandbaby she hadn't known existed, but I knew if anyone could handle it, it would be her. *So much for not breaking anyone else's heart!*

***

After we told Grandma our story and she gave us hugs, kisses, and condolences, we headed back to work. It was dark outside by the time we finished compiling all the profiles; we had gotten to ninety-five percent completion.

This success was due solely to Grandma and her gal pals. They'd all dove into the task at hand, getting every piece of available information about each of the victims.

While we were waiting for the algorithm to do its thing, Dad called. He'd gotten worried when he hadn't heard from Grandma all day. We assured him all was okay and that Grandma would be on her way home shortly. Since it was dark, Jack was going to drive her home; we'd take her car to her tomorrow. She didn't want to leave until the results were in but I knew that could take hours, so I sent her packing.

However, contrary to the norm, the program spat out the data before the two had barely been gone twenty minutes. I took the page into the other room where I could sit comfortably and review it.

Jack had been right; the killer hadn't appeared to select his victims based on any particular physical qualities. It all came down to hobbies and ex-husbands. If I'd been a betting woman, I would've put my money on two specific things: hockey and alimony. Now, it was time to figure out how to catch the killer before he struck again.

Chapter Four

We spent the next several days devising ways to both lure the killer into a trap and catch him in the act. We all knew it would be a long cat-and-mouse game because he worked up to stealing the women blind; he didn't just do it straight off. While we waited for the details to be finalized, we went about normal business. Mine, of course, was matchmaking.

Tonight, Sara and I were getting ready for a double date of sorts. Well, not exactly a double date. We offered a special service to our clients when they made their first match. If they were too nervous about the date, whether because of personal or security concerns, we offered to either set them up on a double date or to shadow them while on their date.

Our current client, Tiffany, had opted for the latter. We—two of us versus one because just one person peering over someone's shoulder was creepy—would be going to the same restaurant as Tiffany and her match and watching to make sure everything was A-Okay. If at any point she felt unsafe she could text us a keyword and we would step in to rescue her.

The one rule we had ... just because they didn't like him didn't mean they could use us to get out of the date. In the instance they just didn't like the guy, they had to put on their big girl panties and excuse themselves without our assistance.

Just like the need for background checks, we had come by this rule the hard way. Too many women had taken advantage of our "keyword" to get out of a date just because they were too chicken to say no thanks when they didn't care for their gentleman caller. After several wasted hours doing others' dirty work, we put our rule into effect. Now, the women had to feel unsafe in order to use the texting option.

If they wanted a get-out-of-jail-free card, their only option was the double date, which wasn't with us, but with another client that had also been matched and wanted to use that option as well. Then, they could use each other to get out of the date if it was an epic fail.

Granted that didn't always end well either. For instance when one client's date was going well and the other client's was not. Still, it would provide them with some assistance in faking whatever ailment necessary to duck out early.

As I finished dressing, I prayed that tonight would go smoothly. At least we would be getting a nice meal out of it; Tiffany's date had selected TajRa for dinner. TajRa had to-die-for Indian food. I especially enjoyed eating there because I didn't get to do it often; Jack didn't care for that particular cuisine.

The doorbell rang as I was sliding on my shoes. Sara was here, on time as always. I quickly headed for the door, grabbing my clutch on my way.

Sara eyed me up and down and smiled. "Well, don't you look snazzy."

"Why thank you!" I curtsied before closing the door behind us. "You don't look so bad yourself."

Sara had donned a *churidar kameez* outfit—skinny pants under a loose, colorful tunic. For once her hair was a tame chestnut color. Normally Sara expressed herself through her hair, both in style and color—possibly because she was a hairstylist and it was easy for her to do herself.

My hair still sported the cut Sara had given me after she had accidentally melted a chunk of my long hair off with a flat iron. She'd been mortified at the faux pas but had given me an amazing short hairdo in its place. We had, however, changed it just recently by adding in some highlights.

After we were both situated and belted into the car,

Sara drove us to the restaurant. We checked in with the maître d' and were seated. Both Tiffany's and our tables had been pre-reserved, so we were strategically placed to be able to intervene if necessary.

The restaurant interior did a wonderful job of making you feel as if you had been transported to India; deep, rich colors were used on the walls and linens, melodic tones escaped the hidden speakers around the room, and the bouquet of incense—with hints of nutmeg, clove, cinnamon, and coriander—wafted through the air and tickled your nose.

We purposefully arrived a short while before Tiffany and her date so we could get most of our dinner eaten before they arrived. This way if we had to respond to her SOS, the entire evening wouldn't be a total loss; we would've at least gotten a nice meal in.

Just as we finished polishing off our dinners, our couple arrived. Tiffany wore a skin-tight, black minidress whose hemline barely hit her mid-thigh. I would've said, "Oh, to be young again," but the truth was, even in my twenties, I would've never worn such an outfit.

Her date, Randall, wore a long sleeve dress shirt which he'd paired with a pair of faded denim jeans. Not the fanciest of attire, but at least they weren't rags, I'd give him that.

They were escorted to their table and Tiffany gave us a subtle head nod when she located us. I gave her a smile in return.

As they took in the menu and made their dinner selections, Sara and I decided to share an order of *Annam-Kobbari Parvanam* (Rice and Coconut Kheer). This wonderful Indian-style rice pudding dessert was accented with cardamom, coconut, raisins, and cashews. It had just the right amount of sugar to curb our sweet tooth.

After ordering, we checked back in on the young couple. When I glanced back at Sara her face mirrored my own; we were both dumbfounded. Both Tiffany and Randall were sitting at the table concentrating on their phones. Not a single word was being exchanged as they waited for their food to be served.

To make things even more mind-blowing, at one point I swore he actually texted her something *instead* of just speaking to her. I guessed this because at the same moment his phone let out a *SWOOSH* sound, her phone made a *DING*. She read the text, laughed, and for a split second their gazes locked.

"Are you freaking kidding me?" Sara asked.

"I know, right?"

"No wonder these young adults can't find anyone to marry. They can't even manage an actual verbal conversation."

"You're preaching to the choir, sister," I said, as my gaze swept around the room and took in all the other twentysomethings who were mirroring the actions of our couple. "It boggles my mind."

Sara chuckled and took a sip of her drink.

Since all seemed to be under control with the date, I figured I could move on to other topics. "We finally got back the results on our mystery killer."

"Really?" Sara set down her drink. "What did they say?"

"It appears the police were right about his not choosing victims based on physical appearance. The algorithm's only matches were based on hobbies and previous relationships."

"How so?"

"Well, it appears the victims thus far all share two things in common: a love of hockey, and each one was receiving a hefty alimony from a previous marriage."

"Interesting." Sara tapped her freshly manicured fingernails on the table while she reflected on the information. After a few moments, she said, "Do you know who that reminds me of?"

I tilted my head. "Who?"

"Julia!"

My mouth flew open. "Holy cow! You're right. I knew something kept tickling my brain when I saw the results, I just couldn't figure out what."

Julia was not only a die-hard hockey fan, she'd been married not just once, but three times—a large alimony being paid out to her for each one.

"So, what does Jack plan to do with the information the algorithm spit out?" Sara asked.

"He hoped he could talk us into throwing a T.A.F.T.

sponsored hockey night at Love Bites for the next Winnipeg Jets game in order to try and draw out the killer," I said.

Even though they were no longer the Atlanta Thrashers, fans still loved to watch their once ago hockey team when they were playing. So, I thought Jack's plan was a good one.

"Do you really reckon this guy would come to an event where you are expected to be a member first to attend?"

The waiter arrived at that moment and placed our dessert in front of us; both Sara and I picked up a spoon and dug in.

"This wouldn't be like our normal mixers. We would just be sponsoring the event. There would be no strings for whoever comes, and no one has to either be part of our agency or become part of our agency."

"Um ... that might fetch too sizeable a crowd for what you all are trying to do. Wouldn't it?" Sara dabbed her mouth with her napkin.

"I agree it would bring in a large crowd, but we should know the majority of those who would walk through the door, so we can weed them out," I said. "Also, because we scan licenses at the door versus just doing an eyeball check, Jack will be able to use that data to run it through the police system and verify identities. Any people we don't know, we'll target."

"How are we supposed to keep track of who the

women hook up with without letting them in on the plan?"

Before answering, I took a quick moment to peek over at the couple to ensure they were still doing ok. I noticed their food had arrived and each of them had finally put their phones down and were now actually having a discussion. Tiffany and I made eye contact and she beamed. I took this as affirmation all was going well enough. I diverted my attention back to Sara.

"Because this is a multi-city task force effort, the police will be using all their resources and planting undercover female officers and detectives in the room as potential dates. A few of those will possess exactly the right criteria to meet the killer's requirements." I took a drink of tea to wash down my last bite before I continued. "In addition, they will specifically seek out the 'questionable' people that walk through the door, i.e. the men we don't know, aren't from the state, or who are new in town."

Sara put down her fork and leaned back. "That still seems like a lot of people who could connect without us knowing."

"Well, that's where we come in. It will be up to the five of us: me, you, Grandma, Julia, and Becky—our new receptionist—to try to steer our known clients together," I said. "It will take some homework on our part to run extra match checks through the system so we know who to connect."

"I know we are trying to help catch a killer, but won't that hurt our bottom line if we are giving away matches and dates for free?"

"Possibly, but if any of our T.A.F.T. clientele find a match that works, that will be a positive on our match statistics which is a marketing win for our success factor."

"Makes sense." Sara shook her head in acknowledgment before scoping out Tiffany's table. "It appears like they're about ready for dessert."

I glanced back and saw she was right. I grabbed my phone and shot a quick text to Tiffany, asking if she was all good. She quickly shot back that she was fine, and that we were free to exit.

If something derailed after this point it would be up to her to figure out a solution. We didn't do door-to-door service. At some point, you had to trust your client's instincts as to whether their date was a threat or not. By the time dessert arrived, that should be fairly clear.

I waved at the waiter to close out the check and after we had paid we made our way back to Sara's car. It didn't take long to reach my house.

"Thanks for pitching in tonight," I said.

"It's part of the job." Sara chuckled.

"Yeah that's true, but Julia was up-to-bat. You helped her out of a pickle. I know she really wanted to go out to eat with Devon at Junior's. She loves that place."

"What are friends for? I mean I know they just met, but it really looks like Julia might've found one who will stick around for a while."

I reached over and gave her a quick hug before getting

out and heading inside. Next item on the agenda: plan a party to bait a killer. *Fun times!*

Chapter Five

By mid-morning on Friday, Becky had finished putting together the flyer for the hockey night event. We'd found a hidden gem in Becky. She'd been straight out of college when we'd hired her on.

Even though she'd had no on-the-job skills, we all saw something in her that led us to take a chance and hire her. We were lucky we had. She was not only a wonderful receptionist—friendly, kind, helpful—she was quick, intelligent, and exceptionally creative.

The final flyer was marvelous. The girl had serious artistic skills. It would most definitely grab people's attention.

I emailed the file to Jack for his approval regarding the

date, time, and location just in case something had changed that I was unaware of. It was only a few minutes later that I received the go-ahead to distribute. I emailed the copy to Julia and Sara, so they could post it at both Love Bites and Runs With Scissors. Becky would post at the local hot spots: Where You Bean and McClellan's pro-shop.

The basic idea was we'd flag any men who showed up at the event that met our criteria, and then the undercover females will rotate around until they've connected with them all. If any of our four plants—the ones who had both of the criteria—were asked for their phone numbers they would give out the number of a burner phone, and we would make a note of who they gave them to. We would then add that person to the list for further research.

A special note would also be made of any clients that showed up who met both criteria: hockey lover/alimony receiver, so we could ensure we pointed them in the direction of someone we knew was not the killer.

After that, it would just be a matter of following the relationship while dropping all the appropriate breadcrumbs to entice the perp to act. Once we had him on the line, it was all about reeling him in and catching him in the act of both stealing money and attempting murder.

I squashed down the fear I felt at knowing we had no other choice but to involve regular Belmont citizens—and our clients—in the ploy, but it was the only way we would be able to make the sting work. Jack reassured me that no one would get hurt. Hopefully, at least a few would make a match and it would be all worth it in the end.

As I perused the rest of my email, my intercom buzzed.

"Callie, there is a new client here to see you," Becky's voice floated up through the intercom.

I quickly scanned my calendar and didn't see any appointments left for the day. "Did she make an appointment?"

"No. She hoped she might just be able to drop in and speak with someone."

Not wanting to pass up the opportunity to acquire a new client, I quickly straightened my desk as I spoke into the intercom. "Go ahead and send her back."

I chuckled as I slid the rest of the loose papers into my drawer. Prior to living with Jack, my surroundings were always pristine and organized. I guessed he was starting to rub off on me a little.

I opened my office door at a soft knock. Becky and a young, ginger-haired girl who I gauged to be in her mid-twenties stood in the doorway. She was average at best in the looks department, sporting pale skin and tons of freckles to prove she earned her red hair naturally and not through a bottle.

"Callie, this is Pepper."

I smiled and held out my hand. "Hello, Pepper. Come on in."

Becky said a quick goodbye as Pepper gave my hand a swift shake before moving into my office and taking a seat.

"Thank you so much for taking the time to see me," she said. "I know I don't have an appointment."

"It's no problem at all. I'm glad we had some time available to answer your questions."

"Me too."

"Well, let me start by giving you some information on T.A.F.T.." I swiveled in my seat and grabbed a welcome packet out of my filing cabinet. I slid it across the desk. She reached over and picked it up. When she did, I noticed she had a unique, ember orange and fire-engine red flame design painted on her acrylic nails.

"Those are fascinating nails!" I exclaimed. "Wherever did you get them done?"

Pepper angled one of her hands down, so I could better see her nails.

"Thank you." A slight blush crept up her face. "Actually, I did these myself. I'm a graphic designer, so I'm pretty good at drawing things. My friend, who does nails for a living, applies the acrylics and then I paint them myself."

"Wow! You're sure talented. I can barely polish my nails, much less do a design as intricate as that."

Pepper's face lit up at the compliment. "I promise it took a lot of practice."

"Well, they're fabulous!" I leaned back in my chair. "So, what is it you want to know about our services?"

Pepper set the packet back down on my desk. She averted her gaze and her blush increased. "Actually, I've read all this online. I did some research before I came over."

"That's wonderful."

Her gaze snapped up. "It is?"

I gave her as warm a smile as I could to try to soothe away her embarrassment. "Of course it is. That will save us some time on paperwork. Can you think of any other questions?"

"Do you take clients like me?"

I tilted my head. "What do you mean, like you?"

"Well ... not beautiful." She dropped her gaze to the floor and the blush once again colored her cheeks. "All the T.A.F.T. client pictures online have beautiful women in them. I don't really fall into that category."

I cringed inwardly knowing she was accurate in her assessment. Not because we only allowed attractive people in, but because most of our clients—and the residents of Belmont—were just that, beautiful. I longed for more average clientele, probably because I fell into that category and knew firsthand how hard it was to compete against beautiful women.

"Don't you worry, Pepper. Our goal is to help *everyone* fall in love no matter their appearance or income level."

She let out a breath. "That's good to hear. Finances were going to be my next question. I'm not certain I can afford your services, but I'm desperate to find love."

"There's no need to worry about the finances. We can find something to make it work for you."

A smile stretched across Pepper's face. "That would be amazing! I've tried on my own and I just can't compete with the women in Belmont. I'm tired of being lonely."

"Now, Pepper, let's be frank with one another." I softened my tone, so she knew this wasn't a statement of criticism, but it was a statement to get down to the truth of things. "Why do you perceive you can't find love?"

Pepper chuckled. "We could start with my name. Do you know how hard it is to traverse through life with a name like Pepper Walsh?"

"Probably as hard as having the name Calla Lily Bloom."

Pepper's head jerked up with a start, her eyes open wide.

I shrugged. "Yep, that's right. My full name is Calla Lily Bloom."

I could see the wheels spinning in her head before she let out a huff, slumped down into her seat, and whined, "Well, at least you get to shorten yours to a cute nickname. No matter how you do mine, it's just silly."

"That's where you're wrong. Your unique name is an advantage as an adult, and you should use it as such."

Pepper raised a single eyebrow. "An advantage?"

"Absolutely. Your name is an easy icebreaker. If you use it right, you can make it as silly or un-silly as you choose. Humor does wonders for catching a guy."

Pepper poised herself a tad bit straighter in her chair and unfolded her arms. "I hadn't really thought about it like that before."

"Don't you worry. If you sign with us, we'll work with you to overcome all your fears and perceived obstacles, so you are set up for success."

Excitement flashed across her face as she wrung her hands, clearly trying to contain her joy.

"What do I need to do to get signed up?"

***

After I finished up with Pepper, I headed home. It was once again time for our weekly meal at Dad's house. I knew Grandma was on pins and needles waiting for us to spill the details about our upcoming operation. I just hoped that the news didn't upset my father. He was not a fan of me being involved with helping the police compile data, much less plan a sting operation.

Jack was waiting in the drive as I pulled in. He quickly got into the car and buckled up.

"You ready for tonight?" I asked, turning my gaze to him. "You know Dad's not going to be happy no matter what you say."

"Yep. I've got my Kevlar on." Smiling, he tapped on his chest.

I knew he was joking, but the idea almost had me pulling back into the drive so he could do exactly that, but I knew better. Jack wouldn't do it, and Dad—no matter how angry he got—would never hurt a fly.

This time when we got to Dad's, he wasn't on the porch. Being that we were a few minutes late, I was almost certain he was in the kitchen pacing back and forth, salivating at the fragrance of whatever Grandma had made for dinner. The man had tunnel vision when it came to food; he was like an animal. If he smelled food within a mile, he was ready to eat it.

Jack and I entered the house and headed towards the kitchen. If the sour tang wafting through the air was any indication, we were having corned beef and cabbage for dinner. Based on that, I knew for certain I would find Dad in the kitchen drooling.

As we hung a left into the kitchen, we saw Grandma was in the midst of giving Dad's hand a swat as he tried to lift the lid off the Dutch oven to peer inside.

Jackpot!

"I'm not going to tell you again, son. Keep the lid on the roast or it will get dried out. I'm not serving the kids a dry meal because you can't behave yourself."

I chuckled at Grandma's reprimand. Dad might've been in his late sixties, but that didn't stop Grandma from scolding him when necessary.

"Don't worry, George," Jack said. "We're here!"

Dad's face lit up, and he stuck his tongue out at Grandma—who was facing away, towards us.

"Don't make me send you to bed without dinner!" Grandma chided, without ever glancing over her shoulder. I swore that woman truly had eyes in the back of her head.

Dad blushed before slinking away to take his designated seat at the table. Grandma and I quickly served dinner and we all dove in.

"So, are you going to keep an old woman waiting?" Grandma asked before I even finished chewing my first bite.

Jack smothered a laugh with a cough. While we were on our way over we'd debated when to discuss the details with Grandma. We'd decided it would be best to do it while Dad was eating. This way he would be paying less attention to us and more attention to his food.

"There's not a lot new to tell, Olive." Jack shrugged. "We've posted the flyers for the hockey night event. We'll scan each driver's license as they arrive and then run them through the mobile database that will be set up in the van across the street. As soon as we get any hits on people who meet our criteria—women and men who like hockey, and women who received alimony—we will let you all know."

Before Grandma asked another question, Jack stuffed a fork full of food in his mouth, all the while glancing at Dad to see if he was paying the conversation any attention. *So far so good.*

"Will we get to wear them fancy earpieces, so we can be incognito while you all feed us our info?" Grandma asked, hope clear on her face. It was obvious she had been watching way too many cop TV shows.

"Sorry, Olive. Only our female officers and Callie will wear an earpiece."

"Why is Callie the only one that gets one?" Grandma whined.

I saw Jack begin to reach for the bridge of his nose, but I stopped him with a quick clearing of my throat.

"We need the rest of you to act as natural as possible, and since none of you are used to earpieces, it's best we do without. Callie will let you know when you need to do something with one of your clients," Jack said.

"What's this about Callie wearing an earpiece?" Dad asked, his fork stopped in midair.

Oh, crap! We knew we now needed to tread carefully as the beast was aware of the prey.

"It's nothing, Dad," I said in as soothing a voice as possible. "All I'm doing is making sure our clients are paired with each other. The police will pair up with any newcomers."

Dad rubbed his chin and narrowed his eyes as he flicked his gaze back and forth between Jack and me. I could tell he was debating if he was going to have an issue with this.

"Would you like more corned beef?" Grandma interjected, holding up a piece of beef out of the pot. The aroma of the dish swirled up with the steam that had been released when she'd lifted the lid. Dad's eyes glazed over as he inhaled and stared at the beef in front of him. It took a moment, but finally, he decided the food was more important than asking more questions.

I gave Grandma a large smile and mouthed, "My

hero!"

A wide smile spread across Grandma's face as she mouthed back, "I get an earpiece."

Ugh!

Chapter Six

I checked in with Julia the following week to make sure Love Bites was ready for the party. Julia, the bar's manager and one of my T.A.F.T. partners, informed me everything was set. She'd received the extra kegs of beer and bottles of liquor for the event and the game had been ordered, so they could show it on their jumbo screen and the eight smaller screens scattered around the bar.

Belmont was all abuzz over our party. This made me both happy and nervous at the same time. I didn't want so many people to attend that we wouldn't be able to keep up with identifying and matching them safely, but I did want enough people so that it didn't appear suspicious. I crossed my fingers that one of the people excited about our event was the killer. *Never thought I would say those words to myself!*

Grandma and I were now seated in the precinct conference room along with the rest of the police staff who were going to be a part of the sting operation. Grandma was only here because she'd badgered Jack until he handed over the earpiece she so desperately wanted to wear.

I guessed she was due being she'd saved us from a possible catastrophe with Dad at dinner. However, Jack had told me that he would be putting both Grandma and me on a "special" frequency to only hear things related to our clients. This way we wouldn't accidentally give away anything with our body language. We, of course, didn't tell this to Grandma.

"It's all pretty simple, folks," Jack was saying. "Sheila, Janet, Karen, and Paula will be our big fish. The rest of you will be doing traffic control, keeping the Belmont citizens away from those people who are either from out of town or people who are new to town."

"Do you still want us to talk to the target subjects so they don't get suspicious about only people with their desired qualities speaking with them?" one of the officers in the back of the room asked.

"Good point, and absolutely right. While I don't want all of you to monopolize their time, we do want a few of you to also converse and mix things up. It'll all depend on how many suspects we end up with."

I raised my hand, not sure if I should chime in or not since I was a guest in this meeting.

Jack smirked when he saw my hand in the air. "Yes, Callie?"

"I just wanted to point out that we did try to make the flow of people so it will be in waves during the three hours of the party; we'll do one free beer per person at the start of each hour."

"Won't that make things harder if there are a bunch of drunks running around mixing it up?" a young cadet at the end of the room asked.

"Three beers could only get a light-weight drunk," Grandma guffawed.

Several of the officers chuckled at Grandma's outburst; Jack just pinched the bridge of his nose. Me, I took it in stride. I'd been dealing with Grandma my entire life, so there wasn't much I didn't expect to come out of her mouth given the right opportunity.

"Don't worry," I added, hoping to soothe anyone who was really worried about the topic. "The staff at Love Bites are experts in telling when someone is about to reach their limit. If anyone gets close, they'll cut them off."

"Callie's right," Jack agreed. "The bar's manager, who is also Callie's business partner, is the best of the best when it comes to managing a bar. This is not her first rodeo. It'll just be a touch different on that night.

"Ok, so we're all set. Those of you on the first watch will trickle in during the first half hour; the next batch will be told to come in via your earpiece when the crowd gets large enough to warrant it, so on and so forth. Any questions?"

I glanced around the room and most everyone was shaking their head no. However, one tiny girl in the back raised her hand.

"Question, Tina?"

"Just one, and it might be dumb. What exactly should we wear?"

I locked eyes with Jack and he responded affirmatively; he knew I was the best person to answer this particular question.

"Not a dumb question at all, Tina. Since we aren't going to arrest anyone tonight"—I held up my hand and crossed my fingers—"and all your weapons are staying at home, you'll want to just go with whatever you personally would wear to the event." I quickly added, "Excluding the four of you playing bait."

"So, what should *we* wear?" Sheila asked.

"Based on our research of the victims so far when they attended sporting events, all wore slacks or jeans. Two wore home team jerseys, and one wore a logo T-shirt. Do any of you four own jerseys?"

Two of the four raised their hands.

"Good. Why don't you both wear jerseys, then one of you wear slacks and the other wear jeans. Karen and Paula, go ahead and dress in something casual but try to wear a shirt in the team colors." Jack moved around the room towards me. "If you don't own anything in the team colors, you can buy something and the department will reimburse you."

"Should one of them wear the opposing team colors, just in case he likes someone not cheering for the home team?" Grandma asked.

Jack flicked his gaze at me. "Sounds like a good idea to me."

"I agree." Jack nodded. "Karen, you'll possess the most out-of-town background story, so why don't you wear the opposing colors. Best to cover all our bases."

Karen nodded and Jack turned to Grandma. "Good call, Olive. Way to think outside the box."

Grandma straightened and blushed like a teenage girl at the compliment. "Just trying to be a valuable part of the team, Detective."

Both Jack and I did our best to not laugh. Grandma was taking her role as an undercover agent very seriously. It made me proud knowing I had such an amazing grandmother; she could give any of the other people in this room a run for their money—if they were eighty-plus years old, that is.

The meeting concluded and everyone dispersed to prepare for the upcoming event. Both Grandma and I followed Jack to his office. I smiled when I saw his desk was only partially cluttered. Apparently, I wasn't the only one rubbing off on the other. The first time I'd been in Jack's office I'd found his desk in complete disarray with sticky notes in abundance.

"So, are all the ladies at T.A.F.T. ready for this?" Jack

asked, as he made his way around his desk and took a seat in his chair.

"You bet your bottom dollar, Jackie boy!" Grandma exclaimed.

I put my hand on Grandma's forearm. "Just remember, Grandma, this is serious. It's not a game."

Grandma patted my hand, her demeanor suddenly stoic. "I know, Flower. I'm sorry for letting my excitement get the best of me. We just don't see many interesting things in Belmont."

"Well, sorry to disappoint, Olive, but we hope this ends up being very uninteresting. That means everyone stays safe."

"So, do you want Grandma to meet us at the house tomorrow, or should she and I meet you at the bar?" I asked.

Jack leaned back in his chair and rubbed his chin. At the same moment his expression made it clear he had come to a decision, he leaned forward. "Let's meet at the house. This way I can get you all set up in private and go over things one more time."

"Okay. Well, we'll let you get back to work while we go do one more check with Julia at the bar. I'll see you at home later," I said as Grandma and I headed towards the door.

"Love you," Jack said from behind me.

I glimpsed back over my shoulder. "Love you too."

Grandma and I headed out to the car and drove to the

bar. Julia and Tony, Julia's top bartender, were putting the final touches on everything. Julia was stacking glasses and Tony was arranging the tables and chairs for the best viewing in front of the big screen.

"Hey, you two!" I waved as we entered. "How's it going?"

Tony lifted his gaze as we entered. "We're all good. I'll need to grab some more ice tomorrow on the way in, otherwise, everything is set."

Tony was an absolute doll. He was one-hundred percent masculine yum and also one-hundred percent gay and married to the man of his dreams. You'd never tell by his outward appearance or mannerisms that he was gay, but that served as an advantage in his line of work. Julia never had to worry about him going home with the female clientele, and the male clientele normally thought he was a guy's guy.

"I forgot to ask, who's manning the door tomorrow?" I asked.

Julia, who had finished stacking glasses, gave me her full attention. "Logan and Corbin will be working it. Since we're going to be asking to scan ID's versus just eyeballing them, we'll need an extra body to make sure we don't make people wait too long."

"Good idea. I'm crossing my fingers Jack's tech team won't run into any technical difficulties accessing our system." I made my way over to the bar and took a seat.

Julia regarded me for a moment before she made an

about-face, grabbed a few bottles from the shelf, mixed a drink—which I soon realized was a ginger mojito, easy on the alcohol—and set it down in front of me. "You need a drink."

"You know me too well." I took a sip of the drink and savored the sweet bubbles as they tickled my tongue. Julia knew this was one of two alcoholic beverages I would consider drinking, and that the ginger ale would help to calm the butterflies in my stomach.

Julia made her way around the bar and took a seat beside me. "I assume you're nervous about the party?"

"A little. You never know what could go wrong, but I'm confident we're in good hands with Jack."

Julia made a silly face and made smooching sounds. I swatted at her. "Knock it off; you know what I mean."

"I know, I know." Julia chuckled for a moment before flicking her gaze to Grandma and Tony, who were deep in conversation over Lord only knew what.

Julia pivoted her gaze to me, her lips pressed into a thin line. "Are you sure Olive can keep what we're doing a secret? She isn't the leader of the blackvine for no reason."

I lowered my drink onto the bar and pondered the question. Finally, I shook my head. "I'm sure. She knows what's at stake and she would never intentionally put any of us in danger."

Julia exhaled. "You're right. I'm just being silly. I know she wouldn't ever be so careless. I don't know why I even questioned it."

I reached over and patted Julia's arm. "You're nervous and you have every right to be. It's not every day you bait a killer in your bar."

"That's no joke." A small smile erased some of the worry lines that had moments ago creased her brow.

Just then my cell rang. I dug it out of my purse and answered.

"Hello?"

" ... Hey, Becky. What's up?"

" ... Did she have an appointment?"

" ... Ok. Just stay calm. I'll be right there."

I quickly hung up the phone, slid it into my purse, and hopped off the bar stool.

"Everything all right?" Julia asked. "You just paled several shades."

"It's Evelyn. She's at T.A.F.T."

"Oh shit!"

Chapter Seven

After Tony volunteered to drive Grandma home, I hauled butt to the office. Evelyn Stuart, our most difficult—both because of attitude and age—and, unfortunately, wealthiest client had a habit of showing up unannounced and wreaking havoc equal to a 7.0 earthquake. Her favorite pastime was chewing people up and spitting them out.

Even for the most secure person, she had a way of making you feel six-inches tall and an idiot. She did this by purposefully making it so you had no way to pinpoint exactly what her issue was, or how to solve it; she would change whatever the problem was as soon as you started to guess what it was.

Becky was as good as any one person could be at keeping Evelyn calm for a short period of time. I prayed today it would be long enough for me to make it the distance from the bar to the office.

When I walked into the lobby, both women stopped dead in what they were saying. Becky and Evelyn were in a showdown of sorts; Evelyn was crimson-faced and Becky was pale. Though, given her current state, Becky was still holding her ground. I moved steadily forward, hand outstretched.

"Evelyn. How nice to see you. What can we do for you today?"

Out of reflex I was certain, Evelyn took my hand and shook it. I took advantage to grasp hold, and in as unobvious a way possible, drag her toward my office. I knew if I gave her an opening the first half hour of her visit would be re-telling what wrongs Becky had committed upon her arrival.

I glanced over my shoulder as I made my way back to my office and saw Becky mouth a "thank you" before she sighed, shook her head, and returned to her chair.

I maneuvered Evelyn into one of my guest chairs before going around my desk and taking a seat. Pasting my most pleasant smile on my face, I asked again, "So, what brings you in?"

Evelyn reached into her humongous handbag and pulled out a manila folder, which she slapped down on my desk. "What kind of game are you playing?"

I straightened in my chair and prepared myself for round one of the game; flashes of the hunger games ran through my mind. I made sure *not* to smile at the thought.

"Game?" I asked, tilting my head.

"This"—she reached forward and grabbed the folder back up off the desk and shook it in the air as she appeared to search for words—"asinine list of matches you sent. Is it supposed to be a joke?"

"May I?" I asked calmly, as I reached for the folder. I already knew who was on the list in the folder; I just wanted to relieve Evelyn of any kind of weapon. I did *not* want my death to be from a zillion paper cuts.

She lowered the folder and let me take it from her. I opened it and perused it; I wanted to ensure what I thought was in the folder was accurate before I inadvertently stepped on a landmine.

"I'm very sorry, Evelyn. I don't see the issue; all of—"

"What do you mean you don't see the issue?" she screamed in a tone just short of ear piercing. "All these men are in their seventies."

I let out an inward sigh of relief. For once, the issue appeared to be obvious and fixable. "So, you're saying you would like us to change our algorithm to match you with men in their fifties?"

"Fifties?" she bellowed. "What do you expect me to do with an old man?"

I refrained from banging my head against the desk.

Evelyn was in her late seventies, so to find matches in her age range, much less men in their sixties, was hard enough, but to go younger? Did she expect us to be miracle workers?

"I see. Well, Evelyn, I'd be happy to re-run matches in a younger age group, but I'll give you the same warning we gave you previously: that big of an age difference could lead to men potentially forming relationships with you only to get to your money."

Evelyn scoffed. "Doesn't T.A.F.T. pride itself on ensuring their clients are not taken advantage of?"

I took a deep, steadying breath. T.A.F.T. did, in fact, pride itself on protecting our clients from being swindled. One of the main ways we did this, however, was to make sure they matched within a reasonable age range. It was when people weren't realistic that things got tricky.

"Yes, Evelyn. We do try our very best to make sure everyone is safe. That is why we recommend you stay within a certain age range of matches. However, if you are willing to take the risk, we're happy to—"

"Are you saying you're happy to throw me to the wolves and let them steal all my money?"

Maybe I should let her be the bait for the killer! I immediately admonished myself for letting the thought cross my mind. It was totally inappropriate, but this woman could drive any person to have insane thoughts.

"Of course not, Evelyn. We want you to be happy. However, it's a very tricky balancing act between matching you and ensuring you are protected."

"Is that what you told Wanda Jenkins?"

I jerked back, her words stinging. Wanda Jenkins had been one of our two lessons learned when we had first started our agency. She'd been wooed by one of our pool selection candidates solely for the purpose of taking her for her money.

I saw red and opened my mouth to reply but was interrupted by a knock on the doorjamb. I whipped around, ready to unleash my wrath on the interrupter until I saw it was Jack standing in the doorway. For a moment, I swore he was surrounded by white light and had a halo over his head. My angel come to save me.

Jack exchanged a knowing look with me for the briefest of moments before he switched his attention to Evelyn. "Well hello, Evelyn. It's been a while. You're looking lovely as always. How are you doing?"

Evelyn smoothed her skirt and fluttered her eyelashes, the beet red color of her earlier anger changing to a soft flush.

"You're such a dear," she cooed. "You're looking mighty handsome yourself."

"Why, thank you." His eyes twinkled. "Sorry to interrupt; I was just stopping by to say hello to Callie."

"Well, isn't that sweet." Her words were aimed at me, but her gaze never left Jack. "You were so lucky to land such a fine gentleman."

"Yes. Yes, I was." I smiled. This time it was genuine.

"We were just discussing Evelyn's latest matches."

Jack's eyes widened and his mouth fell open. "I can't believe someone hasn't come along to sweep you off your feet. If I were older, I'd be tempted to do just that."

I cringed. I knew his shocked expression had been fake, and I was grateful for his attempt to sweet talk Evelyn—at least I was until he stepped on the inevitable landmine about age.

I held my breath as I waited for her to react. However, all she did was flinch just the tiniest bit before quickly composing herself. She made no other outward signs the comment had meant anything to her.

"Many have tried." Evelyn preened. "I just want to make sure I find the right one. It's so hard not to compare them all to Willard."

"That's understandable," Jack said. "Willard was an amazing man, but you know he'd just want you to be happy."

Evelyn gazed up adoringly at Jack and folded her hands primly in her lap. "Yes. I suppose you're right."

"Just make certain you're careful, and be safe. There are men out there right now who are searching for women to not only take advantage of, but to hurt."

"Of course. You're absolutely right!" Evelyn bobbed her head enthusiastically as if Jack were speaking the gospel. "Callie has just given me a list of some wonderful men to consider. I'm on pins and needles waiting to see if one of them is the guy for me."

It took everything I had to not roll my eyes nor snort in a very unladylike fashion. Jack moved forward, picked up Evelyn's hand, and gave it a gentle kiss. "I wish you the best. You're in good hands with T.A.F.T.."

I swore that if she hadn't been sitting down, the poor old lady would have fainted on the spot. I hid my smile.

Not wanting to pass up a golden opportunity, I interjected, "So, Evelyn. Are we all set then with the list you currently possess?"

Like a scene out of a creepy *Chucky*-like horror movie, she swiveled her gaze to me slowly. Although she had a smile as sweet as pie plastered on her face, her eyes shot daggers. "Of course, dear."

I started to take a step back but caught myself. "Good. Let me walk you out."

Jack, being the gentleman he was, gave Evelyn his arm, and we walked her to the front door. As the door closed and Evelyn moved out of earshot, Becky spat, "Don't let it hit you on the ass on the way out."

I locked eyes with Jack for a split second before we both burst out in laughter. Becky immediately joined in.

"She's sure a piece of work," Becky said.

"You girls are too hard on her. She's sweet."

That earned him a swift punch to the arm. When I pulled back for another, he put his arms up in surrender.

"I'm just joking!" He took one step back for safe measure. "I know she's a serious pain in the ass. I don't know how Willard lasted so long."

When we finished laughing, we both took a seat in the lobby.

"I'm guessing you are here for more than just to say hello?" I asked.

"My Spidey sense was humming, so I rushed right over to save you from danger!"

I rolled my eyes. "Yes, my hero." Jack gave me puppy dog eyes, so I quickly added, "I'm serious, you're my hero. Five more minutes with that woman and who knows what would've happened?"

"I'm glad my timing worked out well for you, but of course, you're right. I'm here for multiple reasons. One of which is to get a copy of the profiles you created. I'll ask our female detectives to read them over to make sure they can help pair the good folks of Belmont as appropriate."

Without even having to ask, Becky reached into her desk drawer, walked over, and presented a folder to us. "Here you go. This is the latest and greatest. I put the ones on top that like sports and who are likely to attend."

"Thanks, Becky. You're a gem!" Jack took the folder and tucked it under his arm.

Becky blushed as she made her way back to her desk. Not many women were immune to Jack's charms. I forced myself to tamp down a small spark of jealousy. I knew Jack was mine and only mine, but Becky was adorable and personable, which made me subconsciously take pause.

I jumped a bit when Jack kissed me on the cheek. "What was that for?"

"Just because."

I smiled, knowing he had read my worry and was trying to reassure me. He knew my past and that my marriage had ended because my ex had cheated on me with a cute, young blonde. So, he tried to do all he could to soothe my insecurities when he saw them bubbling to the surface.

"So, we should be all set." Jack got up and made his way to the door.

As he headed out—one hand on the door, the other holding the folder—I hollered at him, "Oh. One small hiccup"—I raised my hand, my thumb and forefinger a tiny bit apart in demonstration.

"What's that?" His body went rigid as he waited for the other shoe to drop.

"Grandma's bringing her boyfriend. He wants to work as a bouncer."

Jack—unable to pinch the bridge of his nose because his hands were otherwise occupied—let out a snort, shook his head, and without saying a word moved forward and left.

I couldn't blame him. I mean, what could be said when you're told an eighty-plus-year-old, want-to-be biker was going to play bouncer at a police sting? *What could possibly go wrong?*

Chapter Eight

The night of the party was here and everyone at Love Bites was all abuzz. Grandma's boyfriend, John, had met us at my house so Jack could go over all the rules specific to him. I knew it was going to be a long night when I opened the door to see that John had arrived on his deathtrap—i.e. motorcycle—and wore head-to-toe leather: gloves, boots, jacket, and chaps. Yes, chaps.

"Hello, John." I tried my best to keep a straight face and not laugh at his getup.

"Well, hello, Flower," John said.

My jaw dropped, and I saw a kaleidoscope of red. *Did he just call me Flower?* Unable to see through the veil of anger, I only felt the whoosh of air when Grandma grabbed John by the elbow and yanked him in the door.

"I told you not to call her that!" she hissed.

A warm hand reached up and peeled my fingers from their death grip on the door.

"Breathe," Jack said softly into my ear.

At the sound of his voice, my blood pressure slowly receded, and I calmed. I took a deep, full breath.

"Good," Jack whispered. "Remember, we're trying to avoid having anyone killed tonight. That includes John."

I did a one-eighty and ran smack dab into Grandma who'd been hightailing it back into the room.

"I'm so sorry, Flo"—she stopped herself—"I mean, sweetheart. John was just trying to be nice. He doesn't understand how sensitive you are about your name."

I gritted my teeth. "It's fine, Grandma. Just make sure it doesn't happen again."

"Of course. I promise." She moved forward and gave me an appreciative hug.

"Okay, ladies and gentleman," Jack announced, as he maneuvered us out of the hallway and to the office. "Let's get you all set up and go over the instructions."

We followed him into the office and each took a seat. Jack moved over to the desk, opened up what resembled a sunglasses case, and grabbed out two tiny devices.

"Ladies, these are your earpieces. You can put them in whatever ear is most comfortable. I'd recommend a hairstyle for tonight that will cover your ears. The more they stay hidden, the more useful they'll be." He handed us each a device. "As I mentioned before, you'll hear us tell you when someone is entering the club who is out of town or new to town, as well as a short description in case you aren't able to get a good look."

Jack swiveled back to the desk and opened a duffel bag. From the bag, he pulled out a black T-shirt and a walkie-talkie.

"Here you go, John." Jack handed him the shirt. "You can keep on the jeans you're currently wearing, but you'll need to lose the chaps."

John's face fell as he took the T-shirt. Clearly, he was unhappy he'd be required to change his outfit. I, on the other hand, let out an internal cheer. I *really* hadn't wanted John walking around wearing his current choice of attire.

Grandma grabbed the shirt from him, shook it open, and held it up against his chest. "Looks like it'll fit you just fine, sweetie pie."

I gagged. I wasn't a fan when Grandma used cutesy talk with John.

John gazed down and his expression changed from one of sadness to one of joy. I didn't quite get it until I actually caught sight of the front of the shirt. It had the word "Bouncer" across the chest in big, bold white letters. *Just dandy!* Now we were going to promote the fact that an eighty-year-old man worked the club. *That should go over just peachy with Julia.*

Without bothering to go into the other room, John stripped off his leather jacket and T-shirt underneath. I was immediately blinded by the whiteness of his chest. That was *not* what I'd wanted to see. I immediately flashed back to when I'd helped one of our clients, Gin, do some pictures for her profile. She'd thought "flirty" meant lingerie, so I'd been unexpectedly greeted with a seventy-year-old in a cherry red teddy. The image had been burned in my mind ever since.

When John was finished and once again dressed, Jack handed him the walkie-talkie.

"John, your job is an important one," Jack said. "We need you to guard the back door of the club to make sure no one unexpected comes or goes."

When Jack had told me his idea to put John in the back, I'd thought it was brilliant. Not only would it get him out of our hair, it really would help to ensure that no one would leave out the back without us knowing about it. The only reason someone would go out the back would be for nefarious reasons. *Win-win!*

"What should I do if someone does? Take them down?" John's eyes sparkled with the possibilities. "I'll need some cuffs for that."

Jack, unable to stop himself, pinched the bridge of his nose before answering. "No, John. You will *not* take anyone down. You'll politely let them know the back door is not an authorized exit and then you'll direct them to depart out the front. In the event they give you a hard time or they ignore you, you'll use the walkie to let me know."

Jack moved forward and demonstrated how to use the

device properly. "As soon as I hear you, I'll come back and take care of the situation."

When John realized he'd really just be a door babysitter, the joy faded from his face and it was replaced by a pout. No action would be coming his way this evening.

"Do I at least get a chair to sit on while I do nothing?" John whined.

Grandma quickly moved over to him and patted him on the arm. "Of course, dear. You'll lay claim to the best seat in the house. You know how you love to watch people, and I'll pop by every chance I get to say hello."

Apparently soothed enough, John's face relaxed, and he remained silent. Grandma and I left to finish getting ready, and Jack got the rest of his gear situated. Fifteen minutes later, we headed out the door.

***

We managed to get through the first half hour with no unusual activity. All the patrons thus far had ended up being Belmont regulars. The ones who were single and able to be paired off with someone from the list were dealt with promptly.

All the early and right-on-time fans had snagged their free beer, settled into their preferred game viewing location, and were ready for the action to commence.

Tony increased the volume on the televisions as the first team skated onto the ice. A cheer exploded from the majority of the fans in the bar, being that the first team on the ice was the Winnipeg Jets; only a few boos were heard.

Those who came in during the next wave were hockey fans, but not hardcore enough to need a good viewing seat. They were here for a combination of hockey, booze, and to scope out members of the opposite sex.

In this group, there were a dozen or so people who were either new to town or who were from out-of-town altogether. As they were cleared for entry at the door, Jack's group gave Grandma and me a heads up.

The majority of those folks were male, which made me equally excited and scared, both for the same reason, because one of them could be a killer.

Grandma, Julia, Sara, and I worked quickly to finish up the matchmaking of the people we knew about, so they were taken off the game board and not a piece the killer could work to claim.

Sheila, Janet, Karen, and Paula rotated in to work the marks—the men who came in that we didn't know. As planned, the other undercover detectives and officers made sure to fill in the gaps of time between each introduction so what we were trying to do didn't seem obvious.

I was beginning to relax just as a voice came through my earbud.

"Callie, it's Doug in the IT van. Just a heads up—there is some guy coming in that is specifically asking for you. His name is Michael Spencer."

Just the mention of *his* name took my blood pressure up to an unsafe level. *What was he doing here?* I moved my gaze over the crowd until I spotted him; he was headed straight toward me. I guessed I'd learn soon enough what he wanted. I took in a deep inhale of breath and tried to calm myself. *Don't kick him in the balls, don't kick him in the balls.*

Some might infer I was joking if I told them it was imperative that I chanted this to myself, but I was deadly serious. If I didn't remind myself what I couldn't do, I might very well be tempted to do just that. I deplored my ex-husband with a passion.

"Hello, Mike." I made no move to offer him a hand to shake.

"Callie!" he chirped, in a too happy voice. He moved toward me as if to hug me. I quickly took a step back.

"What's up?" As I gazed into his face, I immediately saw what I was up against. Michael was not only drunk, he was stoned.

The smile on Mike's face fell as he scanned me up and down with his gaze. "What? You're not happy to see me?"

"Happy to see you?" I gritted my teeth. "Why on God's green Earth would I be happy to see you?"

Mike paled and his lips trembled. "Please don't hate me, Callie. I didn't mean to hurt you."

OMG! Is he going to cry?

He stepped forward again, arms outstretched to try to grab me. I put my hands out to ward him off and took another step backward. Unfortunately, this pinned me against the wall. Panic welled up in my gut; I wasn't sure why. Mike had never given me a reason to be afraid of him before, but I'd also never seen him quite like this.

"I'm not sure what's going on here, Mike. You need to get a grip on yourself, go home, and sober up."

"But—" he started to say when Sara came up by my side. She glared at him for a moment before whispering in my ear.

"We've got a potential problem. You see that guy at the bar chatting up Julia?" she said with the slightest of head nods in their direction. "He is fascinated with her and keeps trying to get her to tell him about herself."

Whipping my attention to Sara, I blinked several times and tried to mentally switch conversations, focusing on what she'd just divulged. When I still didn't get the point, I asked, "So, what's the problem? Julia knows how to deal with guys hitting on her."

"The problem"—Sara growled—"is Julia is *also* a perfect match for our killer. Loves hockey, divorced, alimony. Are you picking up what I'm laying down?"

"Shit!" My breath caught as the light bulb not only clicked on but blinded me as if I'd gazed directly into the sun. "We've got to tell Jack."

As if on cue, Jack cleared his throat from beside me. Relief washed over me, knowing he was now near.

"Is everything all right here?" he asked, glaring at Mike while also taking a step in between us.

"This"—I waved at Mike—"isn't the issue right now." I waved Jack in closer. Once he stepped near, I pulled him down toward me and whispered in his ear, "We need to get someone on that guy who's flirting with Julia at the bar. He fits our profile and is being very persistent in getting her info."

Jack pulled back and looked at me, eyebrows arched. Seeing his expression indicated he had the same question I'd had earlier, I pulled him back down and continued, "Julia also meets the profile criteria."

Mike staggered forward and grabbed Jack by the arm, pulling him away from me. "Hey. What's going on here?"

Jack straightened and pulled his arm back, his face going stone cold as he looked at Mike. "What's going on is you're bothering *my* girlfriend."

Mike paled at Jack's death stare, backed away, and raised his hands in surrender. "Whoa, man. No harm, no foul. Right? I was just saying hello to an old friend. We are still friends, aren't we, Cal?"

I gritted my teeth at Mike's use of my even shorter nickname. "We're fine, Mike. You said you needed something?"

Mike flicked a quick glance at Jack before answering, "We can talk about it another time. When you're not busy."

"Sounds good." I maneuvered Mike to a chair in the corner. "Why don't you sit and watch the game for a while, then go home?"

"Okay. But we can talk later?"

"Sure. Later." I nodded.

I turned myself just a bit so I could see the bar, and then waited until Tony noticed me and met my gaze. Tony, with his sixth sense, almost immediately brought his head up and locked eyes with me, one eyebrow raised. I took my finger and ran it across my neck. He nodded once; he knew that meant this patron was cut off from drinks. No words needed.

I walked back over to Jack. "Is everything handled?"

"Yep. I radioed the group and told them there's a potential suspect at the bar trying to pick up Julia."

"What are they going to do?"

"Sheila's going to go to the bar, take a seat, and start up a discussion with Julia. She's going to work in something about it being nice to watch a game without your ex bothering you with questions."

"So, she's letting him come to her?" I asked.

"I thought it was the best move since it appears he might want to be the one to make the first move," he said.

I smiled at Jack, proud he'd realized the best way for the situation to be handled. "Sounds like the right play to me."

Jack flicked his gaze between me and Mike. "Everything okay?"

"Yep. At least for now." I stepped back and tilted my head up. "Perfect timing by the way. You seem to always know when I need you to take care of me."

Jack tipped a fake hat. "Obliged to help, ma'am. That's

my job."

I chuckled, stretched up on my tip-toes, and gave him a quick kiss.

"What was that all about anyway?" he asked.

"Damned if I know. I'm sure I'll find out later." I gritted my teeth. If I got lucky, Mike would forget exactly what he'd wanted to say when his mind cleared from his intoxication. "How are things going with Sheila?"

"He hasn't made a move yet, but he's listening awfully close to their conversation. I'm fairly certain she'll snag him on the hook within the next ten minutes or so."

I laid my hand on Jack's arm. "Do you think he could be the one?"

Jack shrugged. "Never can tell. We'll just need to wait and see."

"What about everyone else? Anyone promising?" I let my hand fall from Jack's arm. As I waited for his response, I glanced over at Mike to ensure he wasn't getting into any trouble. Quickly, I learned I had no worries on that front. Mike was bent over the high table with his head laid down on top of his crossed arms, out cold.

I knew Tony would give him until closing to wake up; after that, he would take his keys, wake him, and send him home in a cab.

"Nothing so far. We gave out two numbers. The rest of the men seemed to not be interested in much more than the game and free beer." Jack's voice broke into my thoughts.

"Well, maybe this was all for naught." I shrugged, as I surveyed the room. About an hour left in the game, then the show would be over. As I finished my once over, I noticed that Grandma was nowhere to be seen. My heart did a quick hop-step.

"Have you seen Grandma anywhere?"

Jack shook his head. "Last I saw her she was giving John a bathroom break. You might go to the back and see if she's still there."

"Okay. I'll do that. Let me know if you need me for anything."

"Will do." He bent over and gave me a kiss.

I left him and wandered through the club in search of Grandma. I threaded my way through the crowd until I reached the hallway at the back. I didn't see either John or Grandma. I swiveled around and peered into the crowd. I didn't see them. I couldn't fathom that either would purposefully leave the back door unguarded. Or at least for their sake, I hoped not. As my blood pressure rose, potentially in suspense of either fear or anger, a thump sounded from behind me.

I swung around and made my way further down the hall, following the noise. As I reached the back door, another similar noise from my left—in a small alcove— snapped my gaze around.

My mouth dropped open as I saw Grandma and John in the midst of getting hot and heavy. Thank God they were both still clothed, otherwise my eyes might've popped out of their sockets.

"Grandma," I shrieked.

John jumped away from Grandma, who quickly straightened her shirt.

"Callie. Did you need something?" Grandma asked calmly, as if I hadn't just witnessed their make-out session.

I opened my mouth to speak, but no words came out. I tried again—still nothing.

"Callie, are you okay?" Grandma asked, taking a step toward me, hand outstretched.

"Don't," I snapped, as I stepped backward. "You two were supposed to be watching the door!"

"We can see the door fine enough from where we was at!" John straightened and puffed out his chest.

"It's best *you* don't speak right now." I glared first at him, then at my grandmother. "You both had a job to do. Everyone else here is taking their role seriously. People's lives could be at stake!"

"That's poppycock and don't you scold me, young lady!" Grandma waved her finger in the air at me. "We both know you gave us jobs that would keep us out of your hair. We might as well not have even come."

"Seriously?" I flicked my gaze back and forth between the two. They folded their arms and made a united front. "If memory serves me right, *you're* wearing an earpiece which no one else at T.A.F.T., besides myself, has, and *you* have access to a walkie-talkie that *no one* at T.A.F.T. has. Please tell me, how exactly are you being left out?"

Grandma ignored my comment and question and instead doubled down. "Just because we're old doesn't mean we're dumb or useless."

I narrowed my eyes. "I'm very disappointed you think I'd treat you that way. All I was doing was trying to keep you safe. But, if that's how you feel, then give me your earpiece and walkie-talkie and leave." I held out my hand and waited.

They exchanged a glance for just a moment before Grandma reached up, pulled out her earpiece, and handed it to me. I took it from her and extended my hand, palm side up, to John. He reached into his back pocket, pulled out the walkie, and handed it over before he started to peel off his T-shirt.

I held up my hand. "Keep it."

I swung around and left, the clank from the door behind me indicating they had exited. I started to walk down the hall and back into the bar, but at the edge of the hallway, I stopped and surveyed the crowd.

There was no way I was going back out there right now; I'd just dealt with too much to step in another pile of doo-doo. I took a deep steadying breath, and, using the walkie, I radioed Jack and told him John and Grandma had to leave and I would be taking up post at the back door until closing time.

I wasn't sure if it was my tone of voice or if he was too busy to get into it, but Jack didn't ask me why they left or why I was watching the back door for that matter. I was pretty certain it was the former and not the latter though, and it reaffirmed in that moment why I loved the man!

***

Jack was right; it wasn't too long after I'd gone in search of Grandma that our man at the bar had slid over to speak with Sheila. By the time the game had ended and the club was on last call, he'd gotten her number and had promised to text to set up a date.

After everyone was gone, we did a quick group huddle. In total, three of the four women had given out their numbers. Regardless, the details of all the men who fell into the unknown category were going to be compiled and sent over to me to run through our algorithm. Better to be safe than sorry. We all headed home and prepared for step two in our plan.

As I drifted off to sleep, the first line of Mary Howitt's "The Spider and the Fly" poem floated through my mind: *"Will you walk into my parlor?" said the Spider to the Fly.*

Chapter Nine

The following morning, I got up and ready earlier than normal; I had a lot to get done. After shoving all the items I needed for the day into my carrier bag, I opened the door to the garage and punched the door opener on the wall.

As the door rolled open, a pair of legs appeared. I took a step back, held the door open with one hand, and grabbed the golf club that was leaning against the wall with the other. I didn't know who the legs belonged to and I wasn't taking any chances.

I relaxed, however, when the door reached the torso of the body and a dark black, well-worn Metallica T-shirt told me exactly who it was. Mike. *Ah, damn! There goes my morning.*

"Mike? What are you doing here?"

Mike raised his hands up in surrender. "I come in peace."

My eyebrows knit together as I tried to make sense of his statement. It was after a moment I realized he was staring at the golf club. I lowered it back down to the ground and moved forward into the garage, letting the house door close behind me.

"Sorry." I frowned. "I didn't know who it was at first."

A grin spread across his face as he tucked his hands in his pockets. "No worries, Cal. I didn't mean to startle you. I was about to ring the doorbell when the garage door opened."

"I'm sorry, Mike, but I'm in a hurry this morning. What's up?"

Mike shuffled from foot to foot and avoided making direct eye contact. "I wanted to talk to you about something. Can you spare just a minute?"

"Won't Ashley be mad that you're here talking to me?" I asked, not able to stop myself.

Mike's gaze snapped up, his brows knit together. "Ashley?"

"Yes, Ashley. You know ... your girlfriend?"

"Oh," he said with a closed-lipped smile. "I assumed you'd heard we'd broken up."

Instead of rolling on the floor with laughter I decided to be adult about the situation. "I'm sorry to hear about that."

"Thanks." His gaze fell to the ground and his shoulders slumped. "It's been tough."

I took a deep breath and swallowed what I wanted to say. Again, I decided to take the high road. "I really need to get going; can you cut to the chase? What is it you want?"

"I want you back." Mike twisted his hands together in front of him.

My mouth fell open and I stared at his forehead, which glinted with the start of perspiration. That had been one of the things that had annoyed me in the later parts of our marriage. He always "glistened" but never actually got as far as sweating. I mean seriously, what human just dews up and doesn't finish by sweat beading up and trickling down their parts? It was just plain weird in my book.

"Cal?" Mike asked, clearing his throat to get my attention.

I whipped around. "Are you serious? You cheat on me, leave me high and dry, and *now*, when she dumps your ass, you want me to take you back?"

"Hey!" he barked. "Who said she dumped me?"

"I don't care who dumped who." I put my hands on my hips. "All I care about is you getting out of my way so I can get to work. I've got tons to do today and no time to spare, much less spend it continuing this absurd tête-à-tête."

Mike opened his mouth but then shut it. Clearly, he was at a loss for words. Good. Maybe that would get him out of my way sooner than later. Not waiting around to find out, I moved toward my car, got in, and started the engine.

When I caught a glimpse of him in the rearview and noticed he was frozen in place, I honked the horn and slowly pulled out of the drive. He jumped as if I'd snuck up on him. He hopped to the side as I got close. Once clear of the door, I pressed the garage door controller to close it.

I wanted to just drive off, but I didn't want to chance Mike might take advantage and sneak into the house. Why would he do that? I didn't know. I just wasn't willing to take the chance. As it finished closing, I gave Mike a quick finger wave and drove away. The girls were going to get a laugh out of this for sure!

***

Traffic ended up being unusually light, so I wasn't too delayed when I finally made it to work. Becky was on the phone when I walked in, so I just gave her a wave and continued on to my office.

After I was settled at my desk, I listened to all my voicemails and began the task of going through my email. The first email I opened ended up being from Pepper. She had apparently had some unforeseen expenses pop up and she wondered if we'd still honor the pricing we had discussed if she waited a month or two to sign up.

I shot her a quick reply letting her know the pricing was good for ninety days, so she had nothing to worry about. She could just send us her completed application and payment whenever she was ready within that timeframe.

My cell phone chirped, announcing an incoming text. I glanced down and saw it was from Dad. Even though I'd known this was coming, I'd dreaded it. I wasn't sure whether Grandma or John had ratted me out, but the deed was done. The text read: *U nd 2 mt me 4 lnch.*

Dad still had a flip phone and hated both talking and texting. Most of the time, reading his texts was equal to solving a riddle; his clever shorthand abbreviations left me stumped more often than not.

I responded back, telling him I was super busy today and asked if we could do it tomorrow. When he responded: *No,* and nothing more, I knew I was in trouble. Deep trouble. I relented and asked where to meet. I *really* didn't have time for this today but delaying it would only make matters worse. Better to just rip off the Band-Aid.

We agreed to meet at McClellan's at noon. McClellan's was a combo golf club/pro-shop/restaurant. The food was a tad bit pricey, but they had to-die-for fried chicken, which Dad absolutely loved. At least I'd get a good meal out of the lecture I was about to receive.

I shot a glance at the clock and saw I only had a few hours to get all the data entered that Jack had given me. So, I quickly set out to work. I decided to start with the men who had taken/given a phone number to one of the undercover officers/detectives.

I opened the algorithm program on my computer and the first file folder. I quickly entered all the data from the man's driver's license. In addition, the police had provided a visual description from the video surveillance cameras. Not that anyone ever lied about their height, weight, or hair color on their driver's license, right?

When I was done with that, I entered all the likes/dislikes that the officers had gathered while they'd flirted with the men, plus all the data the IT group had gathered from their online search of the men. They'd scoured Facebook, Snapchat, Instagram, and Google.

It would take a while for the profile to generate any kind of real data from the algorithm program, so I continued on to the next file. By the time I finished entering the data for the fellows and answering all the phone call interruptions, it was time to head out to meet Dad. McClellan's was on the other side of town.

***

Dad was already seated at a table when I arrived. Like a true gentleman, he stood and pulled out my chair when I reached the table.

"Hey, Dad!" I stood on tip-toes to give him a quick kiss on the cheek. "I'm so glad you asked me to lunch. I know it hasn't been that long since we caught up, but it feels like forever."

"You can cut the crap, Lily," Dad—who had started calling me by my middle name when I was a child—said. "We both know why we're here." Cutting to the chase was how my dad rolled.

As we lowered ourselves into our chairs, I hoped for a momentary reprieve by ordering, but I noticed there were no menus; this meant Dad had already ordered for us.

"Sorry, but I don't follow." I folded my hands in my lap and put my most angelic expression on my face. "I didn't realize we had something specific to talk about."

The scowl on Dad's face intensified until it appeared as if he might add more permanent lines to the collection of those already on his face—which he'd earned from age and a life of hard work.

"Don't play games with me. You know very well your grandmother is angry with you."

I let out a huff, crossed my arms, and flung myself back in my chair. "Oh, so you've already taken her side?"

"Stop pouting, young lady. I haven't taken anyone's side. *Yet*," he added.

The waitress arrived at that moment and filled both of our glasses up with tea. Dad's was straight sweet tea; mine was a half-and-half. I'd been trying to cut back on my sugar as of late.

"Thank you." I smiled warmly at the waitress.

As she walked away, my smile melted into a thin line. I peered at Dad. "What exactly did *she* say happened?"

"She told me you treated both her and John like children by giving them 'busy' tasks, reprimanding them, and telling them to go home."

I reached forward and took a long drink of the tea. The iced liquid helped to cool the anger that was beginning to boil within me. I plopped my drink down firmly enough the liquid sloshed, almost splashing over the edge of the glass. "Did she tell you *why* she was reprimanded?"

"You were upset they weren't watching the door the way you wanted them to watch it. She said they didn't do anything wrong."

"First off, what they did was neglect their duties. She might've thought they were given tasks that weren't important, but that isn't true." I leaned forward and put my arms on the table. "While I'll agree they weren't the most significant tasks, they weren't made-up items just to keep them occupied. Had they not been doing them, we would've had someone else attending to the door and the clients."

"But you did reprimand them because you didn't feel they were doing a good job watching the back door?" Dad asked.

"Well, it's kinda hard to watch the door when you're busy making out in an alcove."

Dad's spine stiffened. "They were doing what?"

The waitress, who clearly didn't possess the knack for timing or reading a room, showed up at that moment with our plates of food. It wasn't until she'd set the plates down and got a look at the expression on our faces that she realized her faux pas. She quickly made her exit.

Feeling like being a brat because I'd been forced to even endure this discussion, I moved forward and took a bite of food instead of immediately filling in the blanks.

When Dad cleared his throat instead of taking a piece of chicken and devouring it, I knew he was not pleased with the game I was playing. I decided not to push my luck, so I quickly swallowed and answered.

"When I found them, they were *not* watching the back door. They were in a full-on make-out session in the alcove by the door," I said. "Yes, it's true they would have most likely noticed someone going out the door. However, I'm not certain they would've recovered quickly enough from their ... *entanglement* ... to identify *who* had gone out the door."

"I see." Dad picked up a piece of chicken and took a bite. I knew he was both digesting the food and what I'd just divulged.

Taking advantage of his silence, I continued. "The situation was not a game, and I got angry. I agree I might've gone overboard telling them to leave, but people's lives could've been put in danger because of their actions."

"I told you not to involve your grandmother in dangerous situations, but did you—"

I burst out laughing. "It's not like I had a choice. When does Olive decide who lets her do what? She's like a bull in a china shop. If she wants to be a part of something, then she is. The only thing I had any control over was what role she played. I put her in the one least likely to be in harm's way."

My nostrils flared as I grabbed a chicken leg and took a huge unladylike bite out of it. When I finished, I grabbed a piece of cornbread and smothered it in butter.

Dad must've gotten the hint that I needed a minute to cool down because he remained silent and instead joined me in eating our meal. When we were about done, the waitress appeared and asked if we wanted dessert. Since their dessert of the day was peach cobbler, one of my favorites, we said yes. She cleared our empty plates and left.

After she left, Dad finally interjected. "You're right. I should've known you didn't stand a chance. And, your grandmother should've been more careful doing her job ...
"

I started to smile until I realized he wasn't done speaking.

" ... but," he continued, "you shouldn't have scolded them the way you did or told them to leave. She's your grandmother, and she deserves some level of respect."

"I know Dad, and I'll apologize." I paused when the waitress showed up with our cobblers. She made haste with dropping off the dishes and filling up our tea glasses. "I was just frazzled from my talk with Mike, and Grandma's actions were the final straw."

"What did that SOB want?" Dad asked with a grunt, as he picked up his fork, took a large forkful of cobbler, and started to lift it to his mouth.

"He wants to get back together." I held my breath to see what my dad's reaction would be.

"He what?" Dad yelped and dropped the piping hot cobbler on his chest. He yelped again—this time from the hot cobbler—as he jumped up from the table and did a jig to get the searing food off his chest. A sunburn-like red mark now decorated the blank "v" section that his shirt didn't cover.

The waitress came rushing forward. "Are you okay, sir?"

She immediately attempted to reach up and wipe off the remaining cobbler from his chest. He gently swatted her away and took a step back.

"I'm fine. No need to worry." He smiled reassuringly.

Taking him at his word, she knelt and scooped up the chunk of cobbler from the floor with her towel. Dad lowered himself back down and took a deep inhale of breath. We waited until after the waitress finished cleaning up the spill before we continued with our conversation.

Dad blotted gently at the burn with a cold cloth the waitress had given him. "Why in God's name would that fool fathom you'd take him back?"

I shrugged. "I don't have a clue. If I had to guess I'd say he doesn't really want me back, he just doesn't want to be alone. He's never really had to take care of himself before; he transitioned from his mom, to me, to Ashley."

I gave myself a mental pat on the back for using her

real name instead of one of the ones I'd come up with for her since my divorce.

"What does Jack have to say about this latest development?"

I kept my head down and concentrated on my cobbler.

"You didn't tell him, did you?" Dad crossed his arms and leaned back.

I chewed on my lower lip and avoided his gaze. "I don't see why I need to. It's not like it's gonna happen. What's the point in poking a bear?"

"Well, if you don't tell him you'd better not tell anyone else either, especially your grandmother. If you do and the beans get spilled, he's not going to be happy."

I pondered this for a moment before concluding that Dad was right as always. Could I refrain from sharing the juicy humorous gossip with the girls? Doubtful.

"You're right. I should probably tell him. I'm not sure I can keep it a secret from everyone."

"That's probably for the best, sweetheart." He reached over and patted my hand. "Now, back to this police matter you've gotten everyone involved in."

I moaned, laid down my fork, and reclined back. "What about it?"

"What is your involvement in it at this point? Jack had better be making sure you're not in any danger."

"Of course he is," I said. "The only thing we do now is give the police the data our system compiles, so they can better investigate the potential targets. Everything beyond that is up to them."

"That's it?" he asked, cocking his head.

"Well, I guess I will be giving them some tips on how to run the dates to best lure the killer in. Most of the policewomen are used to taking control of situations, so it might be hard for them to let go enough to hook him."

Dad slumped back and patted his belly. "I guess that makes sense. You'd just better be careful!"

I saw the food-induced coma slipping over Dad's face. I knew he'd better get home soon to his recliner and a nap. I sure hoped Grandma hadn't gone all out for dinner; I wasn't sure Dad could eat any more. I gave him another glance. Who was I kidding? The man could eat six meals a day.

"We'll all be careful. I promise." I crossed my heart. "Now, I really need to get back to work. Thanks for lunch."

I started to walk away when Dad said, "Don't you forget to apologize to your grandmother."

"Yes, Dad," I replied as I headed out of the restaurant to my car. Time to narrow down that search for a killer.

Chapter Ten

It took me most of the afternoon to finish loading all the data into the algorithm. Hopefully, within a few days, we would be able to provide the police with a pathway to better identify the most likely suspect. Once we knew more about who that might be, T.A.F.T. could create a game plan for the best way to reel in the fish without him realizing he was even on the line.

My gut told me the gentleman Sheila had hooked up with, Paul, was the prime suspect. He'd seemed way too interested in learning details specific to her past divorces and had laid on the sympathy thicker than sorghum on a biscuit.

His license indicated he was thirty-eight and from

New Mexico. The online data the police had found indicated he was divorced, no kids, and loved animals. His profile picture was him with a large black Labrador Retriever named Charlie.

Based on this information, I jotted down a few notes on the file folder to share with Sheila. While I assumed he would work the divorce angle into the dialogue to play the "I've been there, I know how you feel" card, I thought Sheila could take the lead and talk to him about his love for animals and ask him to take her to the local Mexican restaurant for dinner.

If he was a New Mexican worth his salt, he'd hate the Mexican food here because it was not pork green chili based. I'd learned this fact from a high school friend who had grown up in Albuquerque. She'd always had a conniption fit because we didn't serve Hatch green chili, nor did we smother our burritos. To each his own, I guessed.

We didn't know how much of the killer's backstory would be true, so it was best we test out some of it to see just how much of a snake he really was. So far, the information the police had been able to find out about him had been scarce, which led me to believe his past changed with each mark.

Finished with that task, I went back to my email to see what I had missed. Most of it was junk, so I was able to delete it and move on. One of the last items was Julia's monthly advice column. She'd warned us that this month's article would not only be more serious than normal, it would be longer because she felt it best not to cut this one short. I deferred to her expertise on the subject since she'd been married numerous times, and truthfully not all relationship stumbling blocks had any humor about them. I opened the file and read the article:

YOU DON'T JUST GET THE GUY...

First comes love, then comes marriage, then comes ... the in-laws! *Dun, dun, dun.* Before you take the final leap and go all in on your relationship, make sure to meet each other's families. It goes without saying: "You don't just marry the person; you marry the family too!"

While a few rare individuals don't care what their families think and/or are estranged from them entirely, the majority of people will bring their family baggage into the relationship with them. If you're lucky you'll both get along just fine with the in-laws, or at least well enough to get by.

However, in the event you can't stand them or they can't stand you, you need to decide if you want to deal with the drama for a lifetime. It's hard enough to keep a relationship together when all you're fighting is one another. Throw in the opinions and needs of family and there's a whole new circus in town.

This could be as little as the burden of

babysitting, to things as big as lending money. Being willing to give and take is essential if success is in your future.

So, friends. Be sure to dip your toe into the water and make certain it's a temperature fit for diving in and staying for a long while.

This public service announcement is provided to you by T.A.F.T.

After reading her column, I knew something had shifted in her relationship with Devon. Not sure if that was good or bad. Julia had learned firsthand how family affected relationships; the topic had reared its head during her second marriage.

I'd been not only grateful but lucky that Jack and I had both gotten along well with each other's family.

Closing the document, I shot Julia a quick thumbs-up to tell her I'd read the article, and I was all good with it. She didn't need my approval, but we all tried to give our input on anything business-related.

That task done, I leaned back in my chair and rubbed my temples. Completing the next two items on my checklist was *not* going to be fun. I hoped Jack would take the Mike situation in stride and only be annoyed. So, that shouldn't be too hard. Grandma on the other hand ... she was going to make me grovel no matter how much of the circumstances were her own fault.

Meditating on it for a few minutes, I decided my first move was to call a meeting with the girls. A large cup of tea and some advice would come in handy if I was going to make it unscathed through my next two adventures. I texted Julia and Sara and luckily they were both free and could meet me at Where You Bean in thirty minutes.

***

The luscious aroma of coffee beans and the hiss of milk being steamed greeted me as I entered WYB. For once, it wasn't overrun with patrons. I wasn't sure if it was because of the time of day, the storm that seemed to be coming our way, or just plain luck. Whatever it was, I was grateful. It would make it easier to chat with the girls if it didn't require talking over tons of noise.

I gave the room a once-over and saw that Julia had already snagged us a table at the far corner. It was the perfect place to brainstorm. I headed to the counter where I ordered my normal drink, but in its smallest form. I was still filled to the brim with the food I'd had earlier. The only thing I lacked was the caffeine I was about to ingest.

As I was picking up my order from the far end of the counter, Sara made her way in—her now neon pink hair shone like a beacon on a dark night. She was on the phone, so she only gave a small finger wave to acknowledge me as she made her way to the register. Knowing it would be a few minutes, I headed toward Julia to take a seat.

"Hey, you. How's it going?" I asked.

"It's going." I noticed her normal smile was lacking.

"That good, huh?"

Julia just shrugged and took another sip of her drink. I started to probe further into the subject when Sara came to the table. She dramatically slung her handbag over the back of the chair before dropping down into it.

"Boy oh boy. What a day!" she exclaimed.

"You can say that again," I said. Julia said nothing.

Sara tilted her head a bit, raised one eyebrow, and scrutinized Julia. She had picked up on the vibe Julia had been sending out. Normally, Julia would be the first to chime in when Sara left an opening, but all she did today was stare into her drink. Something was clearly up. Sara shot a glance at me, her one eyebrow still raised. I shrugged; I was stumped too.

"Well ... " Sara jumped in to break the silence. "It sounds like we've all had a heck of a day. Callie, since you called this impromptu meeting, how about you go first? I assume you want to give us updates on the party?"

"Yes and no," I said. "There *is* an update, but mostly I need some advice."

"Why don't you get the update out of the way and then you can dish on your drama," Sara recommended.

"Ok, sounds good." I crossed my legs and leaned back. "So, as far as the update, I've entered all the data the police gave me and am waiting for the program to spit out some information. As soon as it does, we'll get together and devise a plan for how to move forward, if any of the matches end up being killer worthy."

I reached forward, grabbed my drink, and took a long sip. The warm sweetness of the tea comforted my nerves.

"Easy enough," Julia said, clearly snapping out of her thoughts and tuning into what was being discussed. "So, what do you need advice on?"

Setting my drink back down, I continued on. "That's a two-parter as well. First, I need to know how to handle a situation with Jack."

"Jack? I thought things were all good with you two?" Sara asked.

"They are, but I need to tell him something and I'm not sure how he'll take it. Thus, I need advice on the best way to do it."

Sara settled back in her chair and crossed her arms. "I guess that will depend on what you need to tell him."

"I need to tell him that Mike wants to get back together."

Julia choked on the drink she'd just taken. "You've got to be kidding!" She took a napkin and dabbed the drops of coffee off her chin.

"Nope." I shook my head. "Apparently, Ashley finally dumped his dumb ass and now he's trying to come crawling back to me."

"You're not seriously considering it?" Sara screeched.

The sound that came out of my mouth was reminiscent of a snorting pig. "Hell no! I wouldn't take that man back if he was the last living thing on the planet."

Julia giggled. "So, what's the issue?"

"The issue is I know I need to tell Jack just so he doesn't hear about it any other way. But, I'm not sure how he'll take it. I assume he'll just blow it off and be annoyed, but I'm not certain. What do y'all think?"

"In my opinion, you're spot on," Julia replied. "Jack knows you can't stand Mike, not to mention what he did to you, so I'm sure he'll just brush it off. Granted, I'm not sure what he might say to Mike the next time he sees him ..."

"Ditto," Sara said. "I agree with Julia. I don't envision you really need to worry about that item. So, what's number two?"

"It's Grandma." Both of the girls inhaled a deep breath. As if the universe also agreed with the weight of the revelation, a thunderous crack sounded overhead from the oncoming storm. We all jumped just a little.

"What did you do?" Sara asked.

"*I* didn't do anything." I sounded whiney even to myself.

"Well, clearly if you need advice, then you did *something*." Julia smirked.

"Geez," I snapped. "Way to back me up."

As if reacting to my anger, the thunder snapped again several times. This time the lights flickered.

Julia put her hands up, deflecting my anger. "Whoa there, tiger. I'm not saying it was all your fault. I just know when you two tangle, normally you both can take a share of the blame."

I looked over at Sara, who just shrugged. "She's right, you know."

I gazed outside for a moment and watched as the light drizzle of rain transformed into sheets.

"Fine," I muttered. "Maybe I did do something. But it was mostly her fault."

"And ...?" Sara drawled the comment out, asking it in the form of a question, which was her norm.

"At the party the other night, I caught her and John making out in the back alcove instead of watching the door. I got pissed they weren't doing their jobs, so I told them so" I paused. "And then I told them to leave."

"Ouch!" Sara flinched.

"How come this is the first we've heard about it? I didn't even realize they'd left early," Julia said.

"I was embarrassed about how she behaved and didn't want anyone to know." I blushed.

"And ...?" Sara added, clearly knowing me well enough to gather I hadn't laid all my cards out on the table yet.

"And"—I gave her a glassy stare—"I guess deep down I was also embarrassed about how I handled the situation. Even if they did something wrong, I shouldn't have told them to leave."

"So, that's why you need to talk to Olive? To apologize?"

"Exactly."

"Oh boy. She's gonna make you grovel!" Sara clucked

her tongue. The sound—tongue stud against teeth—raced down my spine like nails on a chalkboard. Seeing the cringe on my face, Sara ceased clucking.

"That's what I'm afraid of." I frowned.

The door to WYB swung open as several patrons made a mad dash out to their cars, and one person rushed inside toward the counter. The gust of wind that entered when the doors opened blew the paper napkins from the condiments station, lifting them up and sending them flying all around the store. The baristas rushed around the counter and hurriedly grabbed at them as they floated to the ground.

Julia, Sara, and I all reached around us and picked up the ones that had landed in our vicinity. We handed them over to the girls, who promptly put them in the trash can. As they finished picking everything up, a figure made its way over to our table. When it reached us, it lifted its hands and moved its hood down. That's when we were all able to see who it was. *Well, damn!*

My heart started doing double time as I tried to keep my facial expression steady. I searched Julia and Sara's faces and saw they were doing the same thing. We'd all had the same thoughts.

"Hello, ladies!" he said, a large smile across his face.

Julia was the first to recover, so she answered for us. "Hello. Is there something we can help you with?"

His face fell. "Oh, I'm sorry. I thought you'd recognize me. It's Paul. We met at the hockey night event at that bar. Love something."

"Bites," Julia said.

He tilted his head and blinked several times. "What?"

"It's called Love Bites," Julia said.

"Oh yeah." he shook his head and zeroed his gaze in on Julia. "I'm really bad with names. I remember your name though, Julia."

I metaphorically threw up in my mouth, just a tad, at his poor attempt at flattery. By the expression on Sara's face, she concurred. Julia, always the pro, showed no signs of repulsion and instead said, "Well, I'm glad I'm worth remembering."

"That you are." He shifted his attention to Sara and me. "And who are your stunning friends?"

"This is Callie." Julia pointed to me. "And that is Sara."

"Nice to meet you both. I remember your faces a bit, but I don't think we ever actually met."

I was grateful he didn't attempt to shake our hands or make any kind of physical contact. I was decent at faking basic emotions, but I failed miserably when physical contact was involved. I knew if he touched me I'd either recoil or shudder. Neither would help the police if I tipped him off with my novice move.

"It's nice to meet you too," Sara said, as she gently kicked my foot under the table to snap me out of my head and back into the present. I just nodded a hello and kept it at that.

The thunder boomed again, and the wind whipped the tree by the windows, causing the branches to make an eerie tapping sound against the glass.

"It seems we might have to ride this one out for a few minutes." He peered out the window and then scouted out the room. "And, it looks like they're all filled up in here. Would you ladies mind if I joined you?"

I looked around and was shocked to see that he was, in fact, telling the truth. WYB had gone from a ghost town to the place to be. Clearly, everyone had made a run for the closest establishment possible when the heavens had opened up.

I knew none of us wanted him to sit with us. I mean, who wants to sit and chat with a potential killer, but we really didn't have a choice without being rude.

"You're welcome to sit." I waved at the empty chair to my right.

"Well, don't let me interrupt you. Feel free to keep on chatting like I'm not even here." He took a seat and took a drink from his coffee.

The three of us exchanged a glance and hesitated. There weren't any topics I had to discuss that we really wanted to talk about in front of him. However, I was at a complete loss about what to talk about. Apparently, Sara was not.

"We were just giving Callie some advice on how to smooth things over with her grandmother. They got in to a bit of a tiff."

I gave Sara the evil eye, but didn't interrupt.

"Oh really. So, is one person to blame or is there enough to share?" he asked.

Knowing it would be rude not to answer, I said, "My grandmother was wrong in what she did, but I handled it poorly. My father says I need to apologize for not respecting my elders."

"I see," he said. "What about surprising her by doing a task of some kind that she hates?"

I tilted my head. "I don't follow."

"Like for instance … " He waved his hand in the air. Clearly, he liked to speak with his hands. "When I last had a fight with my mother, I apologized by washing all the windows on her house. It's the task she hates most above all things. Not only did she get an 'I'm sorry', she got a despised task checked off her bucket list."

I didn't want to like his idea, but I did. "That's not a bad idea," I conceded.

"Yeah," Sara said. "At least that way you get to pick which way you grovel instead of letting her do it."

I shook my head. That did make sense and sounded much better than the alternative. "Thanks, Paul. I will most definitely give that a try."

We were all silent when my phone let out a *DING*, letting me know a text had come in. I reached into my bag, pulled out my phone, and read the text. It was from Jack. He was checking to make sure I was okay.

It was at that moment a thought struck. If we were

going to be stuck here with Paul while the weather cleared, why not take the opportunity to question him? This way we could compare the story he gave us now with the story he might give Sheila on their date.

I quickly texted Jack that we were at WYB, we were okay, and I'd start home as soon as the storm cleared enough for it to be safe to do so. Putting my phone away, I noticed the discussion had stalled. I grabbed at the moment to begin my questioning.

"So, Paul. I haven't seen you around before. Are you new to town?"

"Actually, yes. I just moved here from California."

Interesting. First question and he's already telling a different story then he told Sheila.

"Whereabouts?" Julia asked. "A few of my friends live there."

"In Los Angeles. Being that it is such a large city, I doubt we know any of the same people.

"You'd be surprised," Sara chimed in. "You know what they say. It's a small world."

I gave Sara a light kick under the table to tell her to cool it. She just loved to be coy with words. However, in this instance, if he caught on, it could be really bad for a lot of different reasons.

"That's true." he laughed. "So, what do you ladies do?"

I hesitated; it appeared my plan had just been ruined with one strategic question from Paul. The get-to-know-you treasure hunt was a double-edged sword. I didn't want him to know we were the owners of T.A.F.T., but I wasn't sure how to get out of answering the question.

"I'm a hairstylist at a salon in town," Sara piped in. Thank goodness for quick-on-her-toes.

"That must be fun," he said, before returning his attention to Julia. "And, I assume you work at the bar?"

"Excuse me for just a moment," I interrupted. "I need to use the ladies' room."

Without waiting for an answer, I stood and made my way to the restroom. I wanted to take advantage of his attention being on Julia to leave, thus strategically avoiding his asking me what I do. I doubted either Julia or Sara would offer up the details.

I took my time in the bathroom to avoid more conversation with Paul. When I exited, I noticed that the storm had stopped, or at least there was a lull in the activity. I quickly walked to the table to seize the opportunity.

"Sorry to interrupt again, but it appears the storm might be taking a break for a moment. It's probably best if we all skedaddle before it picks up again." I picked my purse up off the chair and slung it over my shoulder. "It was nice meeting you, Paul. Take care."

I noticed the girls had taken my lead and were gathering up their things and saying their goodbyes. As we made our way to the door, I started to turn back around to give Paul one last finger wave.

I stopped mid-motion when I saw the leer he had on

his face. The way he watched Julia as she walked away was downright creepy. He hadn't noticed me, so I quickly turned back around and walked out. He'd just clinched the number one spot on my suspect list. *Julia had better be careful—really careful.*

Chapter Eleven

When I got home, I found Jack sitting in his favorite recliner, reviewing some paperwork. He smiled up at me as I entered the room.

"Whatcha doin?" I asked.

Jack put down the file folder he'd been perusing. "Becky sent over the data your computer program spit out."

I crossed my arms and let out a boisterous harrumph. "I really wish she would have let me give that a onceover before providing it to you. Sometimes the data needs a bit of tweaking. She hasn't been around long enough to determine if it's right just by looking."

"Don't get your panties in a bunch, Callie. I didn't give

her much of a choice. The captain is breathing down my neck for next steps. We need to get a plan formulated for the dates."

My spine straightened, and I felt my face flush. "I don't give a rat's ass what your captain wants. If y'all want T.A.F.T.'s help, then you'll have to wait until we are ready to give it. I'm not going to watch something go wrong because you jumped the gun using inaccurate data."

"Okay, okay!" He reached forward, grabbed me, and pulled me into his lap. "I get it. You're right. I shouldn't have let the captain push me into getting data I knew you weren't ready to give. I promise I'll do better."

My anger melted away. I wasn't sure if Jack really meant what he was saying, or if he was just really good at knowing how to diffuse a "Callie" situation. In either case, I felt better.

"Thank you." I leaned forward and gave Jack a long, deep kiss. The storm that had strengthened again on my way home let out another ominous crack of thunder, making me jump and squeal just a bit.

"Yikes, woman!" Jack lifted me up, tossed me off his lap, and lifted his finger to his lips. Apparently, I hadn't been quick enough to detach myself from him prior to jumping out of my skin.

"Oh crap! I'm sorry." I reached forward and touched his lip, giving it a once-over. "Are you bleeding?"

Jack shooed me away. "I'm fine, Callie."

I felt tears building in my eyes. I couldn't believe I'd

just hurt him, accident or not.

"Hey now." Jack once again pulled me into his lap. "I'm fine."

"You sure?" A tear slid down my cheek.

He reached up and brushed it away. "I'm sure. See … " He pulled me in for another kiss. It was clear immediately that all was okay. If he was injured in any way, he didn't show it. Our kiss deepened, and he slid his hands under my shirt. I felt a buzzing against my hip.

"Either you've developed another talent I'm unaware of, or your cell is vibrating," I whispered breathlessly, as I pulled away.

"Damn it to hell!" Jack exclaimed, as he adjusted me on his lap and dug into his pocket. Seeing he was having a hard time getting a hold of his phone, I got up.

While Jack dealt with whoever was on the phone, I grabbed the file folder that he'd been viewing and gave it a once-over. Unlike Becky, I could tell almost immediately if any of the data was inaccurate.

I'd been the one—with the help of a friend who specialized in writing programs—who'd developed the algorithm we used. Because of that, I was intimately familiar with its workings and its flaws.

Scanning over the first few profiles, I found nothing amiss and also nothing that made me believe any of the men were the one we were searching for. When I got to the third profile, there were a few things that were incorrect. It stated he liked both dogs and cats—which *could* be true, but it wasn't normally the case—and that he was both divorced and widowed. I was guessing these were both instances of being tired and getting checkbox happy. I made a mental note to correct and re-run this profile. With these items fixed, this person was a possibility, though a slim one.

The last one ended up being accurate and a perfect glass slipper match. It belonged to none other than Paul, no shock there; I had a talent for sniffing out fake men. If only this skill had been present *before* my first marriage, I might have saved myself a dose of pain and suffering. However, if I hadn't gone through that then, I wouldn't be here now with Jack.

I lifted my head and rubbed my neck. A glance at Jack pacing back and forth showed me he was still on the phone. The man never seemed to sit still for any length of time. I knew from the crinkle in his brow the discussion was either a tense one or not going the way he wanted it to.

As Jack finished up his conversation, I group texted the T.A.F.T. staff, including Grandma—my first act of absolution—and told them Becky would be sending over the profile for Paul in the morning for them all to review. We needed to begin plotting out a course of action on how best for Sheila to play her part.

I knew Becky would read the text and know that was my cue for her to send the documents without my actually having to send her a second text. It was certainly nice being able to rely on an assistant who could read between the lines.

"Is everything okay?" I asked Jack when he finally hung up his phone.

Jack growled. "They just pulled two of my best men off the case to work a new, unrelated homicide. Now I get to work with two rookies."

"That's too bad. I know how important this is to you, but cut them some slack; everyone has to start out somewhere. It's not their fault they got thrown on this case."

"I know. I know. I'll play nice, but that doesn't mean I have to like it." He huffed and plopped back down in his earlier vacated chair.

"Well, I might know of something that'll cheer you up a bit."

He straightened in the chair and an ornery grin spread across his face. I chuckled. "Not *that* kind of cheering up, you perv."

He let out a full belly laugh before slouching back in his chair. "Ah, shucks!"

I narrowed my eyes. "I was going to tell you that the last profile is a very solid match for our potential killer."

"Who is it?"

"It's Paul. He's the guy who was flirting with Julia. Speaking of him ... " I trailed off.

This time when Jack sat up straight, his expression was serious. "What about him?"

"We kinda sorta spoke to him today at WYB." I held my breath as I waited for Jack's reaction.

"Didn't you all learn from last time?" he snapped. "You're supposed to stay away from the criminals, not invite them to join you at the table for some chitchat."

I cringed at Jack's choice of words. We hadn't exactly invited him, but that scenario had played out. When I didn't say anything, Jack jumped up.

"You've got to be fricking kidding me. You invited him to your table?"

"Calm down. We didn't invite him to our table. We got stuck with him when the storm rolled through. WYB was slammed with people trying to come in from the storm, we had one of the only seats left, and he recognized Julia. So, he thought he'd take the opportunity to flirt."

Jack pinched the bridge of his nose. "Please tell me you didn't give him any information about yourself?"

"Of course not," I snapped. Now getting angry myself, I stood and paced. "I told him nothing, and Julia and Sara only told him basic generic things."

"Such as?" he sneered.

I stopped, turned, and put my hands on my hips. "You'd better change your smartass tone, mister, if you want to continue this little chat."

Jack took a deep breath, opened and closed his mouth several times, then finally said, "You're right. I'm sorry. I'm just worried about you."

"I know. We're all on edge. I promise we didn't tell

him anything important. Julia just confirmed she worked at the bar—which he already knew—and Sara told him she cut hair. She didn't say where."

"Okay, good. That shouldn't cause any issues then."

"Now that you're not being pissy, would you like to hear the good news?"

"There's good news?"

"Yes, there's good news. We asked him where he was from and he said California—Los Angeles specifically."

Jack tilted his head to the side and pursed his lips. "Why's that good news?"

"Dear God, and you call yourself a detective."

Jack crossed his arms and leaned back. "Pot, meet kettle."

I started to reply then stopped. He was right; I was being just as pissy with him now as he had been with me earlier. I moved over and slumped down across from him.

"I'm sorry. That was mean. What I was trying to point out is that he told Sheila he was from New Mexico, and nowhere in our research is he linked with California."

"Oh. I see. So, this will either give us another place to dig up information on him, or it's proof he lies about where he's from as part of his scam."

"Exactly!" I beamed.

"That was smart thinking. Good job."

I didn't throw the compliment in his face because I knew my plan had almost gotten us into the bind Jack had been worried about in the first place. Best not to share that part with him.

"You're welcome."

"Hopefully that's all your bombshells for tonight?" Jack asked. "I'm exhausted."

"Well, since you asked … " I mumbled and wrung my hands together.

Jack drummed his fingers on the armrest of the chair. "Whatever it is, just spit it out."

"I bumped into Mike today"—no reason to tell Jack where I bumped into him—"I found out what he wanted to talk about."

"And?"

"He wants to get back together."

If I hadn't been so worried about what his current facial expression meant, I would've busted a gut. I'd never seen a dumbfounded look quite like it. When Jack didn't respond, I continued.

"It's not like I'd consider it. He's just crawling back because his girlfriend dumped him."

Jack blinked several times before shaking his head. "I know you'd never consider going back with him. I'm just in shock the dirtbag would have the balls to propose such a thing."

I let out a sigh. "I know, right. In any case, it's water under the bridge. I told him not a chance in hell. While Mike might not be faithful, he's not dumb. I'm pretty sure he got the hint."

A devious looked crept onto Jack's face.

"Don't even think about it, mister!" I pointed my finger at him.

"What?" Jack shrugged, but the corner of his lips twitched into a smile.

"Don't what me. I know you well enough to see when the wheels are spinning in your head. Under no circumstances will you discuss this further with Mike or anyone else for that matter."

Jack's smile turned into a pout. "But—"

"No buts. You got it?"

"Yes, ma'am." Jack saluted.

I smirked. "Now that we've got that all cleared up, how about we head to bed and see what other commands you're able to follow properly."

A sly smile slid across Jack's face before he moved forward, grabbed me, slung me over his shoulder, and headed toward the bedroom.

Chapter Twelve

While I ate breakfast the following morning, I thought about what item I could do for Grandma that would get me out of the doghouse. As I laid my bowl and spoon into the sink, the answer came to me: silverware.

Grandma's most prized possession was her formal set of silverware. It had been my grandfather's wedding gift to her and the most expensive thing they'd owned, beyond a house and car, for the first several years of their marriage. While it was her favorite thing to own, it was also her least favorite thing to maintain. Grandma hated polishing silver, and I knew it was due to be done because she'd been complaining about it for the last few weeks.

With my get-out-of-jail task determined, I texted to

see where Grandma was. She responded a few moments later saying she was on her way to the office; Dad was dropping her off for our meeting. Taking advantage of their absence from the house, I swung by and grabbed the set of silverware.

With the wooden box containing all her precious pieces acquired, I rushed over to the local hardware store and dropped it off for polishing. Yes, it was an odd task to be done at a hardware store, but the owner's wife provided the service as a side business.

I personally thought she'd been sniffing the polishing fumes a few too many years to offer such a thing, but who was I to judge. It wasn't like I was going to polish the silver myself. I was desperate, not stupid. Why waste my time when I could pay someone to do it? I even threw in an extra twenty to ensure it was done on the down-low. What Grandma didn't know couldn't hurt me.

With the silver handed off, I hurried to the office to meet up with the girls. I found them all seated in the conference room reviewing papers, which I assumed were the documents I'd asked Becky to give them.

I ducked my head in the room. "I'll be right there. I've just got to drop off my purse in my office and check my voicemail."

"It's about time you decided to show up and help," Grandma snapped.

Clearly, the fact that she'd been invited to assist with the next step in our task had not softened her anger toward me and our situation. I sped into my office, dropped my purse in my desk drawer, and peered across my desk at the phone. For once, the red light that indicated I had voicemails was not lit. Those tasks completed, I returned to the conference room.

"How's it coming, ladies? Do we have any type of outline yet?"

Sara, who was standing by the whiteboard at the front of the room, pivoted toward me. "We were just getting ready to put some bullet points down on the board."

"Is Jack coming?" Becky asked.

"No," I said. "He's leaving this part up to us; he knows it's our expertise, so he will accept whatever we provide him as the reference for how to proceed."

Becky's face fell just a tad. At her look, a twinge of jealousy rattled my bones. Did Becky have a crush on Jack? It wouldn't be unusual for her to be attracted to him—most women give him a second glance—but I would've thought she would have hidden her feelings better, knowing he was my guy.

I hoped I didn't have anything to worry about, but I would keep an eye on it. The last person I'd trusted without question ended up trying to kill me. Not that I believed Jack would act on any advances from her or anyone else for that matter, but I didn't want to even chance him being put in that position to start with. I would nip it in the bud if I felt it was getting to that point. Go after my man and my claws would come out.

I took a seat in one of the open chairs and swiveled to get a line on the board.

"So, where are we starting? What do you want for the board?" I asked.

Sara tapped the marker against her lip and peered at the white space in front of her. "I think we should start with where he takes her to dinner. I know we want a Mexican restaurant, but which one would work best?"

"Well, I'd say we go with something that isn't too crowded. That way it's easy for Jack and his folks to listen in to the conversation with their bag of tricks," I said.

Sara uncapped and took a quick whiff of the dry erase marker before leaning over and writing "Locations" on the board and underlining it.

"My vote is for Manuel's." Sara pivoted back to return her attention to us.

"How about Bueno Comida's?" Julia asked.

Sara nodded, turned, and scribbled the two restaurants down.

"Those are both good ideas, but I thought Manuel's was under renovation since their pipes burst." Becky interjected.

"You're right!" Sara reached up and used the bottom of her palm to wipe the name off the board. "I'd totally forgotten about that."

"Has anyone been to the new restaurant on Belmont Heights Drive?" I asked. "I think it's called Tres Tequila."

"John and I went there a couple weeks ago. It was full

of the college crowd. I think that would be too noisy for what we're after," Grandma added.

I was a tad bit shocked to know Grandma had been there. Normally, spicy food wasn't her thing, much less Mexican food. I figured it had to have been John's idea.

"How about we stick with Bueno Comida's for now and move on to the next item on the list? If we come up with something better along the way, we can change it."

"Sounds good," I replied, as I looked around the room and saw everyone else's heads nodding in agreement.

Sara turned toward the whiteboard and circled Bueno Comida's. Next, she wrote down "Topics of Conversation" and underlined it.

"I think we've pretty much figured those out. They're: dogs, places you've lived, and if he doesn't bring it up, divorces," I said.

"Sheila's in her mid-twenties, so she should have some practice with dating in general. I'd assume she can fill in the rest of the time with regular stuff," Julia said.

"I agree," Grandma chimed in. "As long as she doesn't blow it talking about her career or cop stuff, she should be fine."

I inclined my head in agreement. Jack had told me this wasn't Sheila's first undercover assignment. He felt she was skilled enough to handle the task and any odd turns it might take.

"It's important we remember we're playing a long game here. This killer doesn't appear to just pick up and kill 'em. He gets them comfortable enough that he is able to rob them blind before he covers his tracks by killing them."

"I read in the files that his relationships with the previous women were anywhere from two to four months," Becky added.

"Ok, so if this one is all squared away enough to get the ball rolling, what about the other potential match?" Sara asked.

Everyone in the room pinned their gaze on me. "Since the match was pretty flimsy, Jack is going to have Karen run solo. Not only is she a seasoned detective, she has a degree in criminology and specializes in profiling. If she doesn't sniff out anything off about him, they won't consider him a suspect worth working too hard on."

"If they already had a profiler why did they need T.A.F.T.?" Grandma asked.

My eyebrows shot up. "You do remember you offered it up to Jack after I made a joke about it, right?"

Grandma's face crinkled up and a look of contemplation reflected on her features as she stared off into the corner. "Did I?"

Normally, I would have told her to cut the crap—I wasn't buying her "memory lapse"—but since I was already in the doghouse, I figured I'd better play nice.

"I think the more minds they have on this the better," Julia said. "The last thing we need is another psycho running around killing people."

"Agreed," Sara said.

"Ok, then. If we're all in agreement, I'll call Jack and set up a meeting with him and his team to go over the specifics."

With that finalized I leaned back, propped my feet on the desk, steepled my fingers, and maneuvered my attention to Julia. "So, Julia ... "

Julia cocked an eyebrow and slowly rotated her chair to study me. "Yes ...?"

"What's up with you and Devon?"

Her gaze shot down to the ground. "What do you mean?"

"Don't play coy with us." Sara made her way over to the chair closest to Julia. "We all read your last article for the newsletter. Clearly, something is up in romance town."

"I knew I shouldn't have written that article," Julia grumbled, and she thrummed her fingers one by one on the table.

"Come on, honey," Grandma prodded. "You can talk to us. No judgment here."

Julia groaned, collapsed back into her chair, and closed her eyes. Without opening them she said, "What can I say, the fairy tale has ended. I thought I'd found something real, but all he really wanted was my money."

"Money?" Sara asked.

"Yeah," Julia sighed. "He said his mother needs surgery, but they don't have the money. He asked if I could loan it to him."

"Maybe you're jumping the gun a bit? How do you know his mother's surgery and his asking for money are the only reason he's with you?"

"At first I didn't. But then I started probing for more details. If I was going to give him any money I needed to know what it was paying for. The more I pressed, the more his story changed."

"Changed?" Grandma asked.

"Yeah. First, she needed to get one knee replaced. Now, he says she needs both knees done, and they want to do them at the same time. When I told him it was odd they would do both knees at once and offered to get a second opinion, he got weird."

"Weird how?" I asked.

"He said he couldn't get me her records to get a second opinion. You know my cousin is an orthopedic surgeon."

"That is odd." I chewed on my lower lip as I thought of all the possible reasons for his actions. Some niggling of something tapped at my subconscious, but I couldn't quite grab hold of it.

My heart went out to Julia. It seemed like she always ran into a roadblock every time she thought she'd found her Prince Charming. At one point I'd thought maybe it was all her own doing, subconscious sabotage of sorts. However, the more I heard the details, the more I had to believe it wasn't her fault, or at least not mostly her fault.

Grandma moved over and gave Julia's shoulders a

squeeze. "I'm so sorry to hear that. I know you thought Devon might finally be the one that stuck."

A tear snuck out from underneath Julia's closed eyelashes and slowly trickled its way down her cheek. She reached up, wiped it away, and opened her eyes. "Who knows? Maybe finding forever love just isn't in the cards for me."

"Maybe it's time to take a break and go solo for a while?" Sara asked.

"I think Sara is right," I interjected. "You have tons of other things on your plate right now. I'm sure you can fill up your time dealing with those, and maybe you can check off some items on your bucket list. I know you have been wanting to go back to school and take some more business classes."

Julia let out another sigh. "Maybe y'all are right. It's time to change my focus. I do have a lot of balls in the air right now I'm juggling. And truthfully, with this hot, muggy summer season I'd much rather play with those non-sweaty balls anyway!"

Even though I burst out laughing with everyone else at Julia's comments, I couldn't ignore the voice in the back of my mind that was trying to tell me something. *What in the hell was it?*

Chapter Thirteen

After jotting down all the notes from our meeting, I headed over to the police station to touch base with Jack. For once, someone I didn't know was working the front desk. A new, young male with blond, windblown surfer hair sat at the desk talking on the phone. He looked up as I approached.

"Can I help you?" he asked, as he hung up the receiver.

"Yes. I'm here to see Detective Brown," I said, before quickly adding, "Jack Brown." I'd learned the first time I'd come in search of Jack that another Brown also worked here.

"Sure. Just one second." He picked up the phone

again, then hesitated a moment before returning his attention to me. "Can I say who's here to see him?"

"Callie," I said. I was grateful I no longer needed to use my full name; I wasn't interested in the reveal and reaction game today. One thing I could always count on was a reaction when someone heard my full name. *Thanks, Mom!*

It was only a few moments before I was allowed back to Jack's office. I walked in, closed the door, and made a beeline for Jack, who I kissed quickly on the lips.

"Hey there, hot stuff." I pulled back and made my way around the desk, dropping into one of the guest chairs.

Jack had recently acquired two new chairs after I had pointed out to him how awful the others looked. What once had been cream-colored chairs had ended up covered in stains and duct tape. His new chairs were upholstered in a multi-brown-tone cloth fabric. A much better choice to hide any long-term stains and wear.

As my gaze landed on his bookshelf, I noticed he had also made some changes there. Previously, he'd had a few odds and ends, unframed photos propped up by those odds and ends, and several random books scattered about. Now, the books were neatly placed upright and secured by a bookend, the photos were framed—several included Jack and me at various locations—and the knickknacks were now limited to his favorite signed hockey puck, which was displayed in a plastic case, and a few awards given to him for each of his promotions in the force.

"Hey there, yourself. To what do I owe this pleasure?"

"The girls and I finished up our suggestion list for you. I thought we'd go over it really quick if you have time."

"Actually, your timing is perfect. Whatcha got?" He leaned back in his chair and put his hands behind his head.

I reached into my bag and pulled out the file folder containing all our notes. I placed it on the desk and flipped it open. Thumbing through the pages, I found the summary which I pulled out and slid to Jack.

"We're recommending that Sheila try to get the perp—"

A snort escaped Jack's lips. I looked up and narrowed my eyes. "What?"

"Perp, huh?"

I shot him an icy glare. I knew he thought it was funny when I used television detective slang. What he thought funny, I thought necessary.

Jack pulled his hands out from behind his head and held them out in front of him. "You know I'm just kidding." He then quickly grabbed the summary sheet and made a show of reviewing it.

I chuckled inside. Jack was not the first man I'd brought to his knees with my icy glare, and he wouldn't be the last.

"If you'd stop interrupting"—I lifted one eyebrow—"We're recommending a specific restaurant and topics of conversation to validate the background information your department has acquired."

"So, if he comes back with a different story, like he did with Julia, we have a new direction to research."

"Exactly," I said. "In addition, these should all be safety zones for him. Discussing them and him believing she has the same interests should secure his interest in her."

"Then it's all wait and see."

"Yep. After that, it's a matter of Sheila working her female charms to keep him engaged and interested. If he is the p—" I stopped myself. "Man, you are looking for, we should be on our way for him to rob her blind and attempt murder."

Jack looked this over further before setting it down. "We really appreciate all of what T.A.F.T. has done to assist us in this investigation ... "

He trailed off which I knew meant he had something to add, but either he wasn't sure how to say it or didn't want to deal with the reaction after it was said. Or both.

I leaned back in my chair. "And, or but?"

His gaze snapped up to meet mine, his forehead scrunching up in the middle. "What?"

"Does your sentence continue with an and or a but?" I grinned sweetly.

"I both love and hate that you can now read me so easily," Jack growled and shook his head. "I was going to add, but ... you need to know that this is where your help ends. We can't afford for any innocent bystanders to get hurt in this sting operation. Unless we directly involve you in a process, you are all to steer clear of the suspect, Sheila, and from spreading gossip relative to the two. Am I clear?"

"Loud and clear." I gave a baby salute.

Jack chuckled and shook his head yet again. To someone else, the last part of Jack's statement might have sounded a bit harsh as if he was talking to a child. However, I knew I had earned the question. When I became involved in Jack's last case—as a suspect, then victim—I had ignored Jack's warnings to leave things be and it had almost gotten me killed.

I also knew the part about gossip was directed toward Grandma as she was the queen of all things blackvine. Given our current tensions, I would've rather Jack told Olive herself not to gossip. I guessed I would just pawn it off on Sara or Julia; they knew the situation and would understand why it would be best for the directive to be repeated from them instead of me. Not that Grandma would listen—I mean where do you think I learned how to be headstrong?

Leaving the summary page for Jack, I tucked everything else into the folder before sliding it back into my bag.

"Do you have time for lunch today?"

"No, sorry. I wish I did, but I need to get this information to the task force and have a one-on-one with Sheila to make sure we are all set."

"You'll be home for dinner though, right?"

"Yep. All good there. What's on the menu?"

I batted my eyelashes and let a smirk spread across my face. "I was thinking I'd do something with chocolate sauce."

Jack swallowed loudly, his ears turning bright red. With that thought planted squarely in his mind, I headed out the door.

Chapter Fourteen

It didn't take long for Sheila to talk Paul into a date and get him to agree to Bueno Comida's as the location. Jack had agreed to let T.A.F.T. sit in a van a block over to listen in on the conversation. We were, of course, the experts on dates and relationships.

Luckily, the polished silver mission had been a success and Grandma and I were back on track. Grandma had been thrilled with her newly polished silver and my short apology. She even apologized to me for her make-out session with John.

I was grateful we had mended our fences; had the olive branch failed, this adventure of being crammed into a small van for several hours would surely not have been pleasant. Thank God all was right again!

I felt odd about the win though; being that the recommendation for how to make amends with Grandma may very well have come from a killer, I didn't feel it right to be thankful to him. Darn moral dilemmas.

For this portion of the operation, we wouldn't be able to direct Sheila in the conversation—she wouldn't be wearing any earpieces or wires. We would only be observing and making notes for future dates. There were several reasons for this decision.

To begin with, all first dates were awkward. So, to direct someone to have the perfect first date would be an instant sign something was off. It was best Sheila act as natural as possible. We'd have to rely on both her female and work skills to make the date successful enough to warrant a second one.

Additionally, it turned out that someone on the force was related to the owner of Bueno Comida's, so Jack was able to get a table pre-arranged and a microphone discreetly attached to the spot; both he and our team would be able to hear the conversation.

We all piled into the van and got situated. After we were settled, Jack entered.

"These will allow you to see and hear what is going on inside the restaurant." Jack pointed at the monitors around the van. "As I stated before, Sheila won't be wearing a wire or earpiece. So, this is a watch and listen task. Write down anything you think needs to be addressed and/or anything you think would be good as a next step after this date."

"What if he goes off script and tries something on the date?" Sara asked.

I could tell Sara was nervous because she was picking at her cuticles, which she never did. As a cosmetologist, she felt it necessary to always look her best to her clients; if you're selling beauty, you should look the part even down to your cuticles.

"We have one officer that will be dining in the restaurant and then two outside—one at the front and one at the rear of the building. If he does something, we'll be there to catch him."

Sara let out an audible sigh. Grandma reached over and patted her on the knee. "I'm sure everything will be a piece of cake."

"Will you—" I started to say.

Jack raised his hand and cut me off, his attention shifting upward toward the ceiling as he stood silent for a moment.

"That was the team." He brought his gaze back down to us. "Sheila is set and is heading in. I'll come get you all when the show is over and it is clear to leave."

Jack moved over and gave me a quick kiss before leaving the van.

"What were you going to ask him?" Julia asked, as the door clicked shut behind him.

"I just wondered when we were supposed to leave."

Julia laughed.

"What's so funny?" I tilted my head.

"You two are so cute. Like two peas in a pod who always finish each other's sentences."

"Whatever." I rolled my eyes. "It's not that bad."

I saw the three ladies look at each other before they broke out in laughter. I leaned back in a huff, but on the inside, I was smiling. Jack was indeed the Yin to my Yang.

***

We watched as Sheila walked into the restaurant. Bueno Comida's wasn't too large of a restaurant, so it should've made for easy observation. The walls were dancing with colors: jalapeno greens, fire-engine reds, and sunflower yellows, just to name a few. Mexican artifacts adorned the free spaces around the room, all the while the owner had managed to maintain a non-cluttered feel. Everything was in exact proportions.

Even though I wasn't inside, I inhaled when one of the two servers passed by with trays of food. One contained a smothered burrito and some enchiladas, and the other had some churros and a bowl of fried ice cream. I imagined the warm, peppery smell of cumin found in the main dishes and the sweet, heart-warming scent of cinnamon in the desserts. My stomach rumbled at the thought.

"Is anyone else hungry?" Julia licked her lips.

We all raised our hands and grinned. At that, Grandma

turned around and grabbed the bag she'd lugged into the van with her. She unzipped it and pulled out a baggie.

"Cookies, anyone?"

"Olive, I love you!" Sara gushed.

Grandma, always prepared, handed out the cookies before handing bottled waters to each of us.

"Go easy on the water, ladies," I piped in. "We don't know how long we're going to be here and there aren't any potty breaks."

Julia, who had just chugged a quarter of her bottle, blanched the tiniest bit. She had the smallest bladder of us all.

Now that we were all semi-fed and watered, we turned our attention back to the monitors and watched as Sheila made her way to her table.

In an attempt to both seduce and further stress there was nothing unusual going on with the date, Sheila showed up in a skin-tight black-blue dress. Though it was tight and sexy, it was not inappropriate.

The length of the skirt hit just below her knees and her ample cleavage was sufficiently covered, only a bit of peek-a-boob showed. The female victims to date hadn't been show stoppers or slutty dressers, but they had all appeared to be at least mildly intelligent. Sheila's goal was to try to entice him without turning him off physically and to be smart, without being too smart.

It wasn't too long after Sheila was seated that Paul arrived. He was a tall drink of water, standing at roughly six-feet. Black, straight, shoulder-length hair adorned his head. He'd pulled it back into a single ponytail at the nape of his neck. A few loose strands framed his face. I personally wasn't into men with long hair but that, and what I deemed the "man bun," seemed to appeal to many millennials. From our viewing perspective, we were unable to see his eyes close enough to determine the color, but I knew from his profile that they were a dark gray. We could tell however that he was sporting a five o'clock shadow. His profile had also indicated he was Caucasian, but based on his coloring, I'd guess there was some Italian in there somewhere.

"Oh, he's cute," Grandma purred.

"Geez, Grandma. Aren't your hormones ever going to wane?" I asked, rolling my eyes.

"Only when I'm dead, Flower!"

At one point in my life, I would've been embarrassed by her remarks; it was just odd for someone her age to still ogle men. But now, I was used to it and embraced her uniqueness.

Returning our attention back to the screen, we listened in as Paul and Sheila greeted each other and ordered. It didn't take long to see how smooth Paul was at reeling in women, or just how good Shelia was at both flirting and at being undercover. She hit all the right notes and asked all the right questions.

Sheila weaved in topics to test what we knew about him. I jotted down all the new information for Jack and his group to look up later. Paul spoke of California, New Mexico—he mentioned while eating that the "green chili" was not what he was used to—and Colorado. There was a collective sigh of disappointment in the van when he mentioned the green chili. We'd all hoped to catch him in that lie. During the conversation, he never once mentioned coming down south prior to his recent appearance in our fine city.

He backed up what he stated online and told Sheila he was divorced—granted, the information had never been able to be confirmed. Sheila tried to pull his ex-wife's name from him but was never successful. I knew Jack was going to have to dig further on this topic.

Although Sheila was able to get him to confirm he loved animals, he never once mentioned dogs specifically, much less his beloved retriever, Charlie. Not that loving animals or Charlie were going to get us anywhere, but it was just one more item to validate his truthfulness on our lie detector checklist.

Had we not been purposefully dissecting and questioning his answers, his slips of the tongue when answering the questions would've most likely gone unnoticed or unchallenged. However, because we *were* watching, the few faux pas he made cemented him firmly as a feasible suspect.

By the end of the date, the following details had been logged: divorced, no kids, loved animals, no siblings, from the West Coast areas of the USA, new to town and the

South in general, and small business owner of a tech company.

The officer inside the restaurant that had played the waiter made sure to tag and bag the items Paul had used to dine. They would use these items to test for DNA and fingerprints. Hopefully, those would give more clues to the true identity of the man.

I let out a breath I'd been holding as I watched the couple make their way out of the restaurant; the date had been anti-climactic.

Jack had told us he hadn't expected there to be anything exciting happening tonight. The killer didn't act on first dates; his was a long game. However, that hadn't stopped me from waiting for something exciting to happen. I guess that kind of drama was only found in the movies.

Before leaving Paul at her car, Sheila was able to solidify another date. One very steamy kiss later—the most movie worth moment of the evening—she was on her way home. Fifteen minutes after that, Jack came to the van and opened the doors.

"You're free to go, ladies. Just—" Jack started to say but was interrupted by Julia, who pushed past him with a quick "Thank God" escaping her lips. She made a beeline for the restaurant and I assumed the bathroom.

Jack raised one eyebrow at me and shook his head. I shrugged.

"As I was saying. Remember, everything you

witnessed tonight stays confidential." He took turns making eye contact with each of us and getting a physical head nod.

When his gaze remained locked on mine, I said, "Don't worry I'll make sure to remind Julia."

Jack bobbed his head, moved aside, and helped us from the van. I stayed next to Jack as I watched the girls get in their car. Once Julia was back and in the back seat, Sara drove off.

"So. How'd it go?" Jack asked.

"You were right. Sheila is a pro. She was able to confirm what was what. I left you some notes on the counter. All were small details, but they could be the one clue you need."

"While I hate to know you are once again involved in a case, I'm grateful for your help. Your help has been monumental in positioning us for success."

"I'm glad we can help. I never thought baiting a killer could be so easy though." My brows knit together in a sudden feeling of concern. It *had* been unusually easy to both find and snag the prey.

"Sunshine, don't look a gift horse in the mouth." Jack put his fingers under my chin, leaned down, and gave me a soft kiss. "After this past year, I think we deserve a break."

"You're damn right we do." I maneuvered around and gave Jack a push back toward the van. "I think it's time for a celebration."

Jack chuckled, hoisted me back into the van, and

closed the doors behind us.

Chapter Fifteen

The case against Paul cooled down after the evidence taken at the restaurant had been processed. They had been able to confirm the prints and DNA belonged to Paul, but they couldn't match the partial print recovered at the crime scene to him. In addition, they had been able to account for Paul's whereabouts during each of the murders. So, as of now, Paul couldn't be linked to anything nefarious.

Jack, who'd learned to listen to his gut, made the decision to not give up just yet. They'd come this far, so they would continue on with the investigation until after all of the breadcrumbs had been scattered, just to see what would happen. Better to be safe than sorry.

So, over the last two weeks, things had progressed

forward with Paul and Sheila—even though Paul wasn't available for dates as often as we'd have liked. Based on the newest information, T.A.F.T.'s role was complete for the time being.

With some time freed up, I decided to do some housekeeping. One of our quarterly tasks was to run a report to see how our clients were doing with generating new matches; they got three per month.

I tabbed down my spreadsheet, making note of any women who had not generated their monthly matches. There were several who hadn't yet clicked the "go" button for the current month, and there were four who hadn't done matches for two months in a row. I picked up the phone and called the first client on this list. Client after client had a reasonable excuse for why they hadn't requested more matches. Most were because they were out of town or just plain too busy. However, when I got to the last person on the list, Vanessa, the story was a bit different.

"So, you met someone new on your own?" I asked. This wasn't forbidden or unusual, just not commonplace.

"I did. I hope that doesn't break any rules."

"Of course not, Vanessa. We're happy you found someone regardless of how you found them."

Her exhale of relief was carried over the phone. "I'm so glad. I was going to call you and suspend my account for a bit, but I was nervous how you'd react."

"I'd be happy to go in and do that for you right now.

Just make sure to let us know if you ever want to start it back up or permanently cancel."

As I spoke, I clicked on the appropriate programs on my computer and modified her account. I noted the suspension was due to meeting someone on her own.

"Thank you so much. Believe me, this whole thing is as big of a surprise to me as it is to you. I met Derek out of the blue."

"Well, that's just incredible. Can't question fate."

"I know, right. To think, had I not been running late for the hockey night event y'all planned with a last-minute errand, I would've never bumped into him at the store."

"Oh, so you met him at the store?"

"Yep. Right in the middle of the produce section. It was like a scene out of a movie. I grabbed an orange and caused a landslide. He swooped in and helped me restore things to order."

I sat back in my chair and smiled. It was nice to hear things had worked out naturally.

"So, did you ever make it to the event?" I asked out of curiosity. I hadn't recalled seeing her there.

"Nope. Though I did watch the game with Derek. Come to find out he was also on his way there. Since we hit it off right away, we decided to go watch the game someplace a bit quieter. I just wish he would've stayed for the third period. He ended up having to leave early for something or other."

"I see." The wheels spun in my mind. "Derek's a

hockey lover?"

"He is, but he's not a fan of our team. He actually loves the Colorado Avalanche."

"That's unusual for this side of the U.S.." I sat upright as a teeny tiny drop of unease crept into my gut.

"Well, he's actually from Colorado and just moved here. So, he hasn't come to love our team yet."

"Colorado?" I felt heat rising into my face.

As I waited for her to confirm I'd heard correctly, I opened up Vanessa's profile on my computer and scanned to her history. The bottom dropped out of my stomach when I saw it. She was both a hockey lover and divorced receiving alimony.

"Yep, Colorado. I always swore I could only fall for a Southern gentleman, but a Westerner swept me off my feet."

"So, he's your type otherwise." I thrummed my fingers on the desktop.

"Not really. I usually go for blond hair, blue-eyed, clean-cut guys."

"And Derek isn't a match?"

"He's none of those things. Think tall, dark and handsome romance novel cover. He's even got the long hair!" Vanessa giggled as she recalled his description.

"I'd love to see a picture of you two together!" I held my breath and waited for her response.

"Derek's not really a photo guy," Vanessa admitted, then added, "Actually, he's not much of a social media guy altogether."

"Really. That's kind of odd, don't you think?"

I really wanted to hang up and call Jack to warn him about the situation, but I knew this might be my one and only time to get the dirt on Derek without it seeming sketchy.

"I did at first, but then he told me that someone had tried to steal his identity before. Now he is super careful."

If only Vanessa knew it was possibly Derek stealing identities, not the other way around. At least now it made sense why Paul had shown up late to our hockey event and hadn't been all that free to go out with Sheila; he was splitting his time between women. If he was trying to determine which was the easier mark, he'd pick Vanessa without a doubt. We had to get her out of the picture, quick!

A thought popped into my mind. T.A.F.T. had been contemplating doing a cruise for two drawing for all our clients, to help send one happy couple to further their relationship. Maybe this was the perfect ploy to get Vanessa not only out of the picture for a short while, but out of the country. Normally, I would've run this by both the girls and Jack, but I knew time was of the essence. So, I decided to work on the fly.

"Well, Vanessa. I called for another reason as well. Though, it might disappoint you a bit."

"Really, what's that?"

"We know how stressful dating is, and how you might

lose your connection to your girlfriends while you are knee deep in the search for love, so several months ago, T.A.F.T. put all our client's names in a hat and picked one winner for a two-week gal pal cruise."

"Gal pal cruise?"

I twirled back and forth in my swivel chair as I made up the details.

"Yes. The lucky winner gets to take one of her besties with her on a two-week, all-expense-paid Caribbean cruise."

I knew T.A.F.T.'s original plan had been for one week, but if I needed to personally foot the bill to keep Vanessa away for another week, I would do it.

The sound of Vanessa taking in a shocked breath echoed over the receiver. "Did I win?"

"Well, originally no," I said. "However, the winner, who was supposed to leave next Friday, had to cancel. We've done an additional drawing and are going down the list of winners until we can find one who can leave on such short notice. Your name was next on the list. So, what do you think? Can you and a gal pal go?"

"My work-from-home schedule is really flexible and my best friend is a teacher and it's her summer break, so she should be free as well. I'll have to check and get back to you in a couple of minutes though. Is that soon enough?"

"Of course."

"One other question," Vanessa said. "You said I

might be disappointed. Why's that?"

I stopped swirling and said, "Well, two reasons. First you might not be free and second, you would have to leave Derek for two weeks."

"Give up a man for two-weeks to go on a free cruise? I'm certain I can manage not to shed a tear. Besides, Derek has a really tight schedule and we only get to see each other randomly."

"Okay. Well, give your friend a call and let me know what she says."

"Great! I'll call you right back."

I hung up the phone and waited. I picked up a pen from my desk and tapped it while I continued to swivel my chair back and forth. Less than three minutes later my phone rang.

"Hello?" I said.

"Callie, it's Vanessa. She's in!"

I let out a breath of relief I hadn't realized I'd been holding. "That's wonderful! I'll have Becky send over all the details."

"Great! I'll give Derek the sad news tomorrow night when I have dinner with him."

We hung up and I quickly wrapped up the conversation. As soon as I hung up, I picked the phone back up and called Jack. "Detective Brown," he answered on the second ring.

"Jack, it's Callie."

"Hey, sunshine. What's up?"

I gave Jack the CliffsNotes version of my conversation with Vanessa. When I finished, Jack sat silently on the other end for several moments. A lump of uncertainty built in my throat.

"Jack?" I whispered, unable to stand the silence any longer. "I'm sorry if I handled it wrong, please don't be—"

"Are you kidding me?" he interrupted. "You're a genius. If you were here right now I would kiss you senseless."

"Really?"

"Of course, really! Not only did you just get us a valuable piece of information, you've assisted in steering the situation so that a citizen is safe and our operation can stay on track."

The lump in my throat turned from uncertainty to happy embarrassment at the compliment.

"You said she's having dinner with him tomorrow?" Jack asked.

"That's what she told me. I assume you'll follow her and see who she meets."

"You bet your sweet ass I will!"

Chapter Sixteen

The following day, I updated the girls on what had transpired. Everyone quickly agreed that the cost for the second week of the cruise would come from the T.A.F.T. budget; I almost cried at the support. Now, we all nervously waited for Jack to figure out who Vanessa's Prince Charming was.

If it wasn't Paul, we'd have a new suspect to follow. If it was, then we had a whole lot more questions than answers. Jack had made sure we all knew to stay clear of the situation. While I understood he was over-sensitive to it, I was getting annoyed at being told the same thing over and over again.

I had just hit "send" on an outgoing message I had

drafted when the intercom on my phone rang.

"Callie, Ethan Chandler is here to see you," Becky said.

My calendar, which I had just checked moments ago, had shown no indication of an appointment with anyone. "Did I miss an appointment?"

"No. He was just dropping by in hopes of speaking with you."

"Okay. Go ahead and bring him back."

I hurried and straightened up my desk, tossing my empty paper coffee cup into the trash, and sliding the loose papers on my desk into a pile. Moments later, a soft knock sounded at the door.

"Come in."

Becky swung open the door and motioned the man through. I stood and walked toward him, hand outstretched.

"Hello, Mr. Chandler. What can I do for you today?"

Ethan, a striking man in his early forties with chestnut brown wavy hair, caramel brown eyes, and a sexy grin was a very popular match. At five-foot-nine he was one of our shorter pool selection candidates, but what he lacked in height he made up for in looks and personality.

"Everything is fine." He reached forward and shook my hand. "I was hoping to talk to you about a situation I am having with one of your clients."

I turned my gaze slightly to Becky who just shrugged. It appeared she knew just as much about who he was talking about as I did.

"Please have a seat. Can I ask who exactly you're referencing?" I walked back to my chair and took a seat.

"Evelyn Stuart."

I put on a smile but groaned on the inside.

"Ms. Stuart?" My brows knit together as I tried to determine what possible reason these two individuals had for connecting relative to T.A.F.T..

"Yes," he replied. "You recently told her I was a match for her profile."

I jerked upright and my mind raced. "I did? Are you certain?"

"Well, at least that's what she told me."

The blood pulsing through my veins slowly heated with anger. "She did, did she? When was this?"

"I'd say about two or three weeks ago. It was a bit odd as most of the time I see the people you match me with directly on your website. But, I just assumed I missed seeing it or something."

I knew damn good and well we hadn't run another set of matches after our last conversation. Even if we had, Ethan would *not* have been a match for her no matter how far you stretched your imagination.

"I do apologize, Ethan. I believe Ms. Stuart has gotten confused. We have not matched you with her. Did you by chance actually meet with her, or was this conversation over the phone?"

"It started as a phone conversation, but then we met

in person. I had no clue who she was, so I went ahead and agreed to the date. Needless to say, as soon as I showed up, I knew something was amiss." He wrung his hands together before quickly adding, "Not that I have anything against older women, per-say; it just isn't part of the specifications I agreed to. I promise I did give her a chance to prove me wrong though. But she was so aggressive and … loud."

The corner of my eye twitched, I knew he was being kind with his choice of words to describe Evelyn. "You have our sincerest apologies. I'm not certain what went wrong, but we will look into it." I leaned forward, putting my elbows on the desk. "My recommendation going forward is to only accept invitations through the online portal, not via phone. As you mentioned, that's our standard point of contact. And, if you ever have someone tell you we matched you, give us a call and we'll verify."

Ethan stood and shuffled from foot to foot. "That's amazing. I really appreciate your time. If you can just make sure my criteria is set at under forty-five, and block Evelyn as a future match as a safeguard, that would be wonderful."

Oh, I was going to block Evelyn from lots of things after this stunt; you could bet on it!

"Most definitely, and we will go ahead and waive your fees for the next month as our way of apologizing."

"That's not necessary." Ethan waved his hands in the air. "Just keep that … lady away from me. That's thanks enough!"

I couldn't help but laugh at the look on his face. Evelyn had clearly done a number on the man.

"It *is* necessary, so consider both items done. We wish you the best of luck finding a love connection in the future."

He seemed so nervous I didn't offer to shake his hand; instead, I motioned for the door. He quickly scurried away or at least moved as fast as a man trying to avoid an awkward situation could. I shut my door behind him and leaned against it. Evelyn had just played her last game with me.

I moved to my desk, processed the refund to Ethan, double checked his criteria—though I knew it would be correct—and conference called the ladies. I didn't even have to finish the story for them all to agree we'd fire Ms. Stuart from our agency. No money was worth her drama. She would learn—don't bite the hand that feeds you.

Chapter Seventeen

Jack's team was successful in their mission to identify the man who called himself Derek. Pictures taken during Vanessa's date had given visual confirmation that Derek was, in fact, Paul. They had hoped to get fingerprints or DNA to back up the identity but had been unable. However, the shots were clean enough to both visually confirm all the attributes—height, weight, and hair color were a match—and clear enough to run through their database and get a facial recognition match with the DMV.

Now, it was just a matter of waiting for Vanessa to be removed from the picture and Sheila to go all in. Based on the clinical profile done after Paul was confirmed as being the prime suspect, it was determined money would be his strongest motivation.

So, based on this, the new plan was to have Sheila invite him over to her home—which of course would be staged and not really *her* home—and have some items strategically placed showing her income. They wouldn't be completely out in the open, but accessible enough that even the most amateur of snoops could find them.

The hope was he would take any absence she gave him to go through her belongings and confirm she was prey worth following. A staged phone call was also going to be made while Paul was present in which Sheila would argue with her ex about alimony. If everything went as planned, Paul could console her in a way that would leave an opening for Sheila to spill some financial beans. As long as he picked up what she laid down, all should go as planned.

I would've liked to have been witness to this operation, but I had my hands full. Evelyn was coming in today and I was going to lay the hammer down. Her contract cancellation paperwork sat completed in front of me. I'd had JJ, our attorney, go over everything in detail to ensure that we were within our rights to fire her. He'd confirmed we were, as long as we provided written notice and allowed her to complete her current month and meet her current matches if they agreed.

While I waited for her to arrive for her appointment, I opened Julia's most recent email. She'd drafted the next newsletter article and wanted our opinion.

EVERYONE INCLUDING BIG BROTHER IS

WATCHING YOU ...

Back in the day, the risk of getting caught in a lie depended mostly on how good of a liar you were. Didn't want to go out on a date with a guy ... tell him you had to babysit. Piece of cake! What he doesn't know won't hurt him, or you—unless of course, he catches you red-handed on a date with another guy on the same night you were supposedly "babysitting"!

Nowadays, however, the game has changed. With Facebook, Snapchat, Instagram, and all those other apps out there, the odds of getting caught in a lie—with photographic evidence to back it up—have gone up exponentially.

So, before you lie your way out of another date—or something else for that matter—ask yourself this ... Is it worth the price you'll pay if you get caught?

This public service announcement is provided to you by T.A.F.T.

I responded that I was fine with what she'd written. It was clear she still had some bones to pick with Devon. Although, to my knowledge, she hadn't yet been able to prove he'd been lying to her, I could tell from what she'd written she believed it to be true. At least the topic was on point and valuable to our clients.

I hadn't ever been able to put my finger on what

bothered me about the whole thing, so I decided to just let it go. It was Julia's issue to deal with. If she needed my help any further, I knew she would ask; I had enough on my own plate right now to deal with.

That task done, I looked down at my watch and bounced my foot on the floor. I was so not looking forward to my meeting.

After I'd finished up the paperwork this morning, I had cleaned off my desk of just about everything. While I expected things to go badly, I didn't know how severe Evelyn's outburst would be. So, I thought it best to remove any and all objects that could be used to harm me. Did I really think she would react with violence? No. Was I willing to take the chance? Hell no!

There was no need for Becky to announce Evelyn when she arrived; she was like an elephant in a china shop, her voice loud enough to wake the dead. Not wanting for Becky to suffer, I headed out as soon as I heard the noise.

"Evelyn," I said. "Thank you for coming in. Would you like to follow me to my office?"

I motioned toward the hall before giving Becky a quick glance. Her smile spoke volumes.

After Evelyn and I were settled in our battle positions, I gave her my most pleasant smile. "Evelyn—"

"Why exactly am I here? You know I've got more important things to do than come here at your beck and call."

Taking a deep breath, I counted to five before sliding

the file folder across the desk. "Evelyn—"

"I assume whatever that is, it's for me?"

One, two, three, four … this time I waited until ten before answering. "Yes, Evelyn. That's for you."

Evelyn made no move to take the folder; instead, she crossed her arms and sat back in her chair. I took a deep inhale and clenched my fists just for a moment, hard enough my nails bit into my palms just a bit. The act helped me focus my rage somewhere other than on Evelyn.

"As you'll see *if* you look in the folder … " I slid the folder a little farther across the table, " … you'll see I've provided you with a notice of contract cancellation."

Evelyn jerked upright, the smug smile on her face disappearing. Whatever she'd expected, it wasn't this. "Cancellation contract?"

"That's correct. T.A.F.T. is providing you with formal, written notice that we're ending our relationship with you."

"But why?" Evelyn asked. Color rose up her neck and her eyes darted around the room.

I let my hands relax, and I leaned casually back into my chair, this time a smug smile spreading across my face. "Come now, Evelyn. We both know why."

"You can't do this!" She snorted dismissively. "It isn't against any of your contract terms to date outside of T.A.F.T."

"That's correct. You're always free to try to find love on your own. However, it is *not* acceptable to approach someone with the ploy that we matched you with them."

"Is that what *he* told you? You can't prove it ... It's his word against mine!"

Unable to stop myself, I let out a very unladylike laugh. "The voicemail you left him is all the proof we need. Or, did you forget you left him a short voicemail *before* you actually spewed your lies to him on the phone?"

I flinched the moment the words were out of my mouth. Not because I didn't mean each and every one, but because I had done exactly what JJ had advised against. Making it personal. From the glint in Evelyn's eyes, she saw my mistake and was thinking of how best to take advantage. Steadying myself, I reeled my anger back in and waited for her response.

She sat up, spine straight and a gleam in her eyes. "Sorry, my dear. You cannot use that in a court of law. In Georgia, both parties must consent to being recorded for anything to be considered admissible."

"That would be true had you called him, he answered, and then he recorded you. But you left a message voluntarily, which means you gave consent." I slid the folder across the desk and smiled. "If you don't believe me, you can reference the statute in the documents provided."

The smile slid off her face and her posture slumped slightly. When her gaze once again reached mine, I saw a glimmer of wetness in the corner of her eyes.

"I know what I did was wrong, but you can't seriously think it necessary to go as far as ending our contract?"

The change in temperament was award-winning and

very, very scary. I felt a flashback to last year and watching something similar play out on the face of my previous assistant—right before she tried to kill me. A tremor of fear rippled down my spine at the same time a wave of relief calmed it, knowing I had removed all weapons from the vicinity. I stood, done playing games.

"I'm sorry, Evelyn. What you did was unacceptable and our decision is final. You have until month's end to attempt contact with the matches we already provided you. After that, our relationship is over."

The tears vanished from her face as if they'd never been there to begin with. "You're going to regret the day you did this to me!"

"You did this to yourself, and I promise you, this is one moment in time I will never regret. If you please ... " I opened the door and motioned her out. "I think it's best you leave now."

Evelyn stood, squared her shoulders, and fixed me with a death stare before stomping out of the office. I followed after her, locking the door, and flipping over the closed sign.

"It must've gone okay? You are still alive, and she didn't burn the place down." Becky asked.

"Not yet anyway. Not yet." Becky blanched a bit as I turned and headed back to my office and the mini bottle of chilled Riesling I'd tucked in my desk drawer for just this occasion.

Chapter Eighteen

I was relieved when Friday rolled around and the work week was done. We'd been super busy, and it was nice to take a breath. I rolled down the car window, inhaled deeply, and wove my hand up and down through the wind as Jack drove us to Dad's house.

The smell of fresh-cut grass and wildflowers tickled my nose. I turned my attention to Jack. He looked tired, but who could blame him. They'd been burning the candle at both ends—working in tandem to get Paul to act, all the while trying to tie him to his past deeds.

In addition to Dad and Grandma's cars in the driveway, John's motorcycle sat propped up on its kickstand. *Oh goodie! This ought to be fun.*

Dad had never cared for any of Grandma's boyfriends, but John—with his motorcycle—took the cake. I was surprised John had lasted as long as he had. Normally Dad found a way to make each one run for the hills. At six-foot-four and pushing two-seventy, Dad had a way of scaring people.

I was a smidge less frosty with John than Dad, but my relationship had taken a step back with the whole situation at Love Bites. While I had worked to get Grandma's forgiveness, I'd never once thought about John.

"You okay?" Jack asked from beside me as he shut the engine off. "You just turned a little green."

I shook myself from my current train of thought and shifted my gaze to Jack. "I'm fine. I was just debating what I might be walking into with John. I haven't seen him since I raked him and Grandma over the coals."

"I thought Olive forgave you?"

"She did, but I haven't tried to make amends with John."

"Well, maybe you'll get lucky. He's a guy, which means he won't give the situation a tenth of the thought a woman would."

I grabbed the door handle and opened the door. "I hope you're right. The one thing I was after this weekend was some stress-free time, not more drama."

Stepping up onto the front porch, I stopped dead in my tracks. Dad and John were sitting together, playing a game of checkers. I did a double take.

Neither man paid us any attention as we made our way forward. Dad was in the midst of jumping several of John's pieces and making it to the opposite end of the board, taking the last of John's pieces off the board.

"King me!" Dad demanded.

I walked up behind Dad, leaned over, and gave him a hug and a kiss on the top of the head.

"Well geez, George. You've whooped me again! You're a checkers pro." John winked at me. Dad didn't see the wink as his head was down while he collected all the pieces and slid them off the table into the box.

"You just need to learn how to strategize a bit more." Dad stood and made his way around John toward the front door.

Based on the wink, it appeared John was strategizing just fine. He was just doing it in a different game and Dad hadn't picked up on it yet. I had to give John credit; he learned fast. The two quickest ways to Dad's heart were food and making him feel superior to you in some way.

John stood and offered his arm to me. "May I lead the way, my dear?"

My brow wrinkled, but I slid my arm through his. Maybe Jack was right. Maybe John had never given the situation two thoughts, or he'd already forgiven me. At this point, I'd take either option.

When I walked into the house, I knew something was off, but I couldn't put my finger on it. As we entered the kitchen, the light bulb went off.

"Where's the food?" I asked, as I extracted my arm from John's.

At that Grandma walked into the room. "It's on its way, Flower. We ordered pizza."

The world spun for just a moment as the shock settled in. I snuck a glance back over my shoulder at Jack, whose mouth hung open.

"Pizza?" I asked when my voice finally returned.

"Yep," Dad replied. "The three of us stopped at a new pizzeria the other day, Mangas, and had some slices with tons of meat and veggies. It was mind-blowing! And, best of all, they deliver."

"You three"—I moved my finger from person to person—"went out to dinner together?"

"Olive's not cooking?" Jack squeaked.

"Of course we went out to dinner," Grandma said. "We go out once a week. And with this sticky heat, I didn't feel like standing in front of a hot stove."

Jack walked over to the nearest chair and slumped down. My reality shaken, I moved behind him and put my hand over his shoulder, both in a show of condolence and to help steady myself. I knew Jack was disappointed because eating Grandma's food was one of his favorite activities of the week. I, however, couldn't believe that Dad and John were actually getting along.

"Yeah. It's about time someone catered to Olive instead of her always catering to everyone else." John leaned forward and gave Grandma a peck on the cheek.

Grandma swatted at him. "Don't be silly. You know I do it because I love to cook. Not because anyone expects it."

No longer stunned, my brain started working again. "We know you do Grandma, but I'm glad you decided to take a break."

Jack, whose face was still fallen asked, "When are they supposed to deliver it?"

I hid a smile. Jack had mentioned at least three times on the way over how hungry he was, so I knew he hoped it was coming sooner rather than later. As if on cue, the doorbell chimed.

Dad moved toward the door. A few minutes later, he came into the kitchen carrying several boxes. He set them down on the counter one-by-one. Grandma opened the lid of each box. The scent of all things Italian wafted through the air. My stomach rumbled in response.

"Dig in," Grandma said. "We've got two kinds, plus some salad, and wings."

Jack and I shared a look. Had we entered the twilight zone? First, they ate out, then they had pizza—which neither normally cared for—and now hot wings! *Who were these people and what had they done with my family, and John?*

I shook my head in disbelief. Jack, whose stomach cared more about his hunger than the enigma before us, didn't hesitate to move forward and start piling a plate high with food.

Moving over to the counter, I picked up a paper plate

and bowl and proceeded down the buffet line. After getting a small serving of salad and slathering it in Italian dressing, I perused the labels on the pizza boxes to determine my pizza options. The boxes read The Works (i.e. all the meats and veggies you could ask for) and Mama's Favorite (i.e. pepperoni, mushroom, black olive, and Italian sausage).

I wasn't a huge fan of mushrooms, but I hated peppers and onions. So, I grabbed a slice of Mama's and moved onto the wings. They were large, meaty drummies whose vinegar and Tabasco scent tickled your nose and stung your eyes just a touch. I decided to only take two; I wasn't sure how hot they'd actually be, and if my stomach would revolt.

When I turned to make my way back to the table, I saw Jack had already finished his first piece of The Works and one wing. His eyes were glazed over. I was fairly certain, had I tried to reach out and take something off his plate, he might very well have growled and possibly bitten me. Clearly, he agreed with Dad's assessment that the pizza from Manga's was worth eating.

I dropped down into my chair and took a few bites of my salad. Unable to wait any longer, I lifted my pizza slice, folded it in half New-York style, and took a bite. The cheese melted into my mouth as the taste of oregano, tomato, basil, red pepper, and garlic danced over my tongue. It was as if I'd just taken a bite out of heaven. I groaned.

"I told you it was good." Dad smiled as he wiped his

mouth with a napkin, his three pieces already devoured.

I should've known if he thought it was good, it would be good. I mean, food was his favorite hobby when he wasn't woodworking.

Jack let out a grunt of agreement but didn't stop eating long enough to say anything more.

"I can't believe I haven't heard of this place before now. This pizza is to-die-for."

"Just wait until you try the wings," John piped in. "They're spicy enough to get a kick, but not so much you can't enjoy the flavor."

Needing no further prompting, I picked up my first wing and took a bite. John hadn't been lying. It was spicy without needing a side glass of milk, and the meat was cooked perfectly. I finished the second one in no time flat.

"Before I grab seconds, is there any dessert?" I licked my fingers and tilted my head to look at Grandma.

Jack—who was in the process of lifting a chicken wing to his mouth—stopped mid-motion, an eyebrow arching upward. Clearly, the word "dessert" had gotten through his food-induced tunnel vision.

"Of course there is!" Grandma put her hands on her hips. "You don't think I would serve less than a full meal?"

I didn't need to hear what she'd made. I was all in no matter what. I'd been eating her dessert long enough to know it would knock my socks off. Both Jack and I licked our lips at the possibilities.

"How's your case going?" Dad leaned back and patted

his stomach, his plate now sitting empty in front of him.

Jack, who'd also finished his plate and was in a food coma, blinked several times as if trying to focus. "Good. Good. Callie helped clear an unforeseen hurdle getting Vanessa out of harm's way." He reached over, lifted my hand, and kissed it gently. "And the suspect took the bait we provided and snooped appropriately. He should now believe there is money to be made, or should I say 'stolen.'"

"What are the next steps?" Grandma stood and picked up the empty plates and moved them to the trash can. I would've helped her, but I felt as if that might warrant assistance from a forklift. I couldn't recall the last time I'd eaten so much in one sitting.

"We'll work in a way for him to access her accounts under the ruse of her needing help to diversify her money. Once he has the account numbers and passwords, it will just be a waiting game. Sheila is doing her best to fend off his physical advances, but she's walking a tightrope. It's uncertain how long he'll be satisfied with not getting her into bed."

"Would she do that?" My eyebrows shot up.

"The department would never ask nor expect her to do such a thing."

"That's a tough one," John said. "To lose the chance to catch a killer just because they didn't want to sleep with the perp."

Jack shook his head. "You're right. I've seen some undercover agents go all the way in order to get the arrest.

So, even though it's not part of the job description, many officers see it as being done in the line of duty."

"Well, I sure hope it doesn't come to that." Grandma sat back down. "She seems like such a sweet girl. I'd hate to see her go down that road."

"I agree," Jack said. "I have a gut feeling we won't have to get that far. She's laid out a background of abuse and abandonment. Paul would have to be a complete jackass to push her to go too fast if he were really seeking a long-term relationship. If anything, he might be glad to not get involved. It might make it easier for him to steal her money and kill her without leaving as much DNA evidence to chance."

"So, does that mean you girls are off the hook for helping?" Dad asked, as he shifted his gaze to meet mine, the concern he felt at our being involved clearly etched on his face. It saddened me to know I was the cause of more than one of the recent wrinkles he'd acquired.

"Unless something unusual comes up, we're pretty much clear," I replied. "It's a good thing too. I've got my hands full now dealing with Evelyn. She's making a huge stink over us letting her go. I'm not sure what that old bat is capable of."

"Don't you worry about her, Flower." Grandma stood and made her way to the refrigerator. The three of us at the table all took an expectant inhale. It was like waiting to unwrap presents on Christmas morning. Jack strained to see into the fridge.

"If she causes too much trouble, Gin will step in and cut her off at the knees," Grandma said.

We'd met Gin several months earlier when she signed up with the agency. She was one of our most senior clients. While I'd thought it would take a long time to match her, I was wrong. She'd almost immediately found matches and continued to find them.

No one to date had turned out to be her Prince Charming, but she had her calendar full enjoying the attention they showered her with while they tried to win her over. Our enrollment of selection pool candidates, over the age of sixty-five, had skyrocketed as soon as the word got out she had enrolled.

This is one of the reasons why I had been so irritated with Evelyn. I knew she had options—good options thanks to our spike of new older men. She'd just chosen to be irrationally picky because she didn't want to admit to her own age.

I was glad to have Gin on my side. We'd quickly learned she was the head of just about every women's social club in town. Her family had been in Belmont for generations and had always held the esteemed titles. She could make or break any woman in this town with the snap of her fingers. I reveled in the thought.

"I'm glad she's on our side. I'd hate to go up against her," I said.

"You and me both," Grandma concurred, as she turned from the fridge, a large glass casserole dish in her hands. The only thing I could make out from my angle was whipped cream of some sort.

"What is it?" Dad asked, licking his lips.

"Tiramisu," Grandma said, as she walked over to the counter and worked to put individual portions onto plates. "I thought it would be fitting, being we were having Italian for dinner."

Dad stood and moved to help her. Dad is a true gentleman so he would've most likely done it anyway, but the fact that it was dessert gave him more motivation to act, and to act quickly. I was surprised I didn't see drool coming from any of the men yet.

Dad took three plates, which he handed to the men. I wasn't offended he didn't give me one of the first plates; he knew I was okay with feeding the beasts first.

Grandma brought the last two pieces to the table and sat mine down before me. The dessert was beautiful—a feast for the eyes. Moist Kahlua and coffee-soaked ladyfingers were nestled between layers of a mascarpone cream mixture. Atop the fluffy decadence was a light dusting of cocoa powder. I brought the plate to my nose and inhaled deeply. The rich, full-bodied aroma of the coffee drifted into my nostrils, swirling with the sweet scent of the liquor and filling.

I lowered the plate and took a forkful, sliding it into my mouth. As soon as it hit my tongue, I closed my eyes and moaned aloud. It dissolved like a sweet, velvety cloud. I let it linger in my mouth for just a moment before swallowing. After everyone had polished off their portions, we made our way to the front porch for some fresh air.

The sun had faded and the flickering of the lightning bugs flying back and forth filled the darkness. Cricket and frog songs filled the air with music. Off in the distance, a bolt of lightning flickered across the night sky.

I inhaled and noticed the smell of rain in the air. "Smells like there might be rain coming our way."

"Well, you best skedaddle then, Missy!" Dad said. "Don't need you getting caught in a downpour."

"You're right, George. Besides, I have a busy day tomorrow and really need to get some rest," Jack said.

I was sad to leave so quickly, but I knew it was for the best. Didn't need to get caught in the dark when it started coming down. Roads by Dad's house were famous for washing out when there were quick, heavy cloudbursts.

We doled out our goodbyes and headed home.

"Did that just happen? Are they all friends? Did your Grandmother just *not* cook a meal?" Jack shook his head as if to clear it as he rattled off all his questions.

"Yes." I stared out the window at the oncoming storm. "I do believe hell has just frozen over."

Chapter Nineteen

The next few days passed uneventfully—which I was grateful for. Stress was one thing I was happy to do without.

Jack's people were still watching and waiting for Paul to make his move. I could tell now why Paul hadn't been caught yet—he was extremely careful.

Tonight T.A.F.T. was going to have some fun. We'd been invited to join Gin at the Selina Country Club for its annual wine and dine event.

It included sampling of all the local wineries' newest creations, and food from the most foo-fooish restaurants in town. While I couldn't care less about the wines—less a good, sweet Riesling or Moscato—I was all in on the food.

I loved to eat fancy, new-fangled cuisine. I just didn't care to dress up, act prim and proper, or pay the tab. It was annoyingly painful enough to have to dress professionally for work. Whoever created pantyhose should be shot; Spanx was still out for debate. I hated the mummy wrap but loved the smooth roll-free outcome.

Olive was sitting this one out. Not because she wanted to, but because her doctor had forbidden her to indulge too excessively in either booze or food. Since she knew she wouldn't be able to control her inner gorger, she decided to just stay home. I felt guilty, but this led me to breathe a sigh of relief. Her outspoken ways had a habit of leading to a scene, which I hoped to avoid this evening.

"What do you think?" I twirled around in my new navy-blue dress. The flared skirt swished softly around my thighs.

The soft, linen fabric was overlaid with lace and had a boat neck design. Because it was linen, the arms and neckline were all lace, and the skirt came to just above the knees, the dress was wonderfully cool. This was important because the event would be held outdoors on the patio and lawns of the clubhouse.

I paired it with a small clutch, some pearls, and cute wedge-style high heels. The wedge instead of traditional heels ensured I wouldn't be aerating the grounds as I walked around, and that I didn't turn an ankle.

"You look stunning as always, my love." His eyes twinkled with appreciation.

My heart fluttered just a bit. I didn't think I'd ever get used to being looked at like that.

"What time will you be home?"

"I don't have a clue. The 'official' event is supposed to end at nine, but who knows if that will be the case."

Jack moved forward, slid his hand under my hair to the back of my neck, and tilted my head backward. "Just be careful." He leaned down and kissed me.

My body molded to his, my hands rising to his chest. We spent several minutes enjoying the kiss. When I felt him swelling against my stomach, I pulled back.

"Unless I want to get this dress all wrinkled, I'd best get going."

Jack pulled me back in and kissed me again. "We can just take it off and it won't get wrinkled at all."

I giggled and pulled away, this time also taking several steps backward to ensure we would stay untangled. "That is a tempting offer indeed. However, I don't have any time. I'm already running late."

"Not even for a quickie?" He wiggled his brows up and down.

"We both know nothing about you is quick." I swatted his advancing arms away and turned toward the door. After sliding my feet into my shoes and grabbing my clutch from the side table by the door, I proceeded to my car and the fun that awaited me for the evening.

***

Lucky for me, Julia and Sara had driven themselves to the party, and we weren't carpooling. Had we been, I would've been more than fashionably late. As it was, I met them in the foyer at five minutes past six; the event started at six.

"Well, don't you two look lovely," I said.

Julia wore a loose, red silk gown that flowed gloriously down her tall frame. She'd paired it with some thigh-high, skintight, black leather boots. Only a woman as tall as Julia could pull off such a look and still look fashionable. On me, it would've looked like I was a slut.

Sara—Julia's polar opposite—had tamed her hair to a rich auburn red so dark you wouldn't have believed it to be red until the light captured the highlights. She'd dressed in a steam-punk, two-piece style outfit. The first piece was a sleeveless, knee-length dress patterned with swirls of rich colors. On top of the dress was a fitted black overcoat with tails that almost reached the ground. The length of the jacket helped to lengthen her overall appearance, giving her height. Of course, the six-inch gold stilettos that she'd worn also helped with that. The outfit was classy enough to not be inappropriately out-of-sorts for the event but unique enough to still maintain Sara's signature style.

"You look beautiful yourself," Julia said. "Are we ready to go in?"

Sara and I nodded, and we followed the signs to the party. We exited the building through two large French doors. The grounds were breathtaking. A large stretch of manicured lawn was surrounded by rose bushes of every color. Beyond that was a lush, full grove of trees—which mercifully threw some shade over the event. There was one pathway between the trees. Through the space, you could see the immaculately maintained eighth hole of the club's golf course.

I took in a deep breath, inhaling the mixture of fragrances from the roses. One breath was floral—traditional rose scent—the next held a hint of fruitiness. I would have to ask which roses held the sweeter fragrance. As one who suffered from allergies to anything floral scented, I would love to have a rose bush that I could tolerate and wouldn't send me running for the Benadryl.

Hearing laughter from below, we walked to the balcony's edge in front of us. We looked down and saw all the guests mingling about on the lower level. Turning to the right, we moved down the steps and in the direction of the decadent smell of food.

"Ladies and gentlemen. Can I have your attention?" Evelyn's voice came from the speakers around the patio. "The food tasting is now open, please enjoy yourselves."

I stutter-stepped down the last two steps and my heart sank at the sound of her voice. I didn't realize she would be here, much less be one of the coordinators. *Oh well, I guess I would have to see her sooner or later.*

At the bottom of the stairs was a guest table. As we checked in, I hoped that Evelyn wouldn't notice us.

"I'm sorry, ladies. Can I help you?"

My spine stiffened and my hand froze mid-motion as I was reaching for my guest bag.

"Well hello, Evelyn," I heard Julia say from beside me. "I didn't realize you were running the event this evening."

"I run all the club's major events," Evelyn seethed. "I'm curious as to why you are here. I'm certain you weren't on the invite list. This event is for members and their guests only."

I turned and pasted on my warmest smile. "We were invited—"

"I don't care *who* invited you. I assure you I outrank them!" she spat vehemently enough specks of spittle hit the tissue paper of my gift bag, causing it to darken.

I pulled my bag in closer, unwilling to let her slobber any further on my goodies.

"But Ms. Stuart—" the twenty-something girl at the gift table started.

Evelyn flicked her an angry glance. "Hush, and mind your own business, you dumb girl!"

The poor girl slouched back down into her seat and lowered her gaze. Her face was beet red, and she appeared as if she might cry. My blood pressure elevated a few notches.

"You three con artists"—Evelyn shot daggers with her eyes at each of us individually—"... don't belong here. Take your white trash, fake asses out of my sight before I call security."

"I do believe the only one here with a fake ass is you, Evelyn," came a voice from the staircase behind us.

From the look on Evelyn's face, I thought her head might pop off her body from anger.

We all swiveled and watched as the figure appeared. Like an angel Gin approached, gliding down the staircase. She looked stunning in a satin and chiffon suit. Her hair was artfully arranged in a French bun at the nape of her neck. An air of confidence and superiority wafted around her like perfume.

Oh, this is going to be good!

Evelyn inhaled sharply, her look changing from anger to fear. "Virginia. I'm so sorry. I didn't see you there. I was just letting these ladies know this is a members' only event, and they needed to leave."

"Do they? I'm fairly certain members were allowed to invite guests?" Gin's brows knit together.

"Well … yes … " Evelyn stuttered. "But there are some extenuating circumstances and these particular guests are not welcome here."

"Why's that?" Gin put a hand on her hip and tilted her head.

Evelyn waved Gin's question away with her hand. "You don't need to concern yourself with this, Gin. I have it under control."

"Actually, I do."

"You do?" Evelyn's eyebrows rose.

"Why of course. I mean these ladies are *my guests* … "

Evelyn paled, took a step backward and straight into a drink server who had been frozen in place. The sudden movement caused the girl to drop the tray. Several glasses of red wine flew like projectiles through the air, the liquid landing squarely on Evelyn. It dripped down her head-to-toe white gown, like an artist's painting when color is thrown at the canvas.

Evelyn turned, arms outstretched in horror, her mouth open as she scrutinized what remained of her outfit. "Look at what you've done! I don't care who you are, I'll have your head!"

"No one is going to side with you on this one, Evelyn, no matter how you spin it."

"You just wait and see. I have more friends here than you do. They'll believe any story I tell them over you and your guests. And this one"—She thumbed to the girl at the desk who now had her hands down in her lap—"will say whatever I tell her to if she knows what's good for her."

Gin clucked her tongue. "I'm sorry to tell you, but next time you want to spread your lies, you might want to make sure to turn the microphone off when you're done using it."

Evelyn's gaze fell, and she stared at the microphone in her hand for a moment before Gin's words registered. Moving at slower than a snail's pace, Evelyn swiveled her head and gazed behind her. We all followed along and saw that everyone at the event was silent and watching the action unfold. They'd seen *and heard* it all play out.

Evelyn blanched and dropped the microphone like a hot potato; an ear-piercing screech echoed out of the speakers. Everyone cringed, covering their ears. For a moment I thought Evelyn would pass out. Instead, she pivoted like a woman on fire and ran for the hills.

Gin calmly moved over, reached down, grabbed up the microphone and chimed, "That's all for our entertainment portion of the evening. Please enjoy the food and drinks."

A round of awkward laughter, lots of whispering, and a few golf claps filled the air before everyone returned to what they had been doing before the excitement.

"That was unbelievable, Gin. Thank you for sticking up for us. I wish Grandma would've been here to see it!"

"Me too," Gin concurred.

"I got it on video if you want to send it to her!"

We all turned to see the gal at the desk holding her cell phone out at us, a very large smile on her face.

Chapter Twenty

The blackvine was all abuzz the following day. Sally, the young lady at the guest table, had taken it upon herself to post her video online, right after sending a copy to Grandma. Grandma had apparently "wet herself" she'd bust a gut so hard. Last check, the video was up to twenty thousand views.

I feared that Evelyn would retaliate against the poor girl and sue her, so I put in a call to JJ. He concluded she didn't have any grounds to sue, but he would call Sally and give her his info just in case she was and needed assistance. I thanked him and told him we'd help pick up costs up to one thousand dollars if necessary. No reason she should pay the full price for something we had a large part in, even if we were in the right.

Of all the things that surprised me the most from the situation was our influx of sign-ups for ladies over sixty. Apparently, after everyone found out that two of the higher society ladies, Gin and Evelyn, had felt it okay to join our agency, they should also be free to do so without recourse. I just hoped our pool of men in the proper age group was both sufficient and sufficiently medically supervised. It's one thing when younger people go at it like rabbits; it's another thing entirely when you throw in age and Viagra. Grandma—who threw out her hips getting hot and heavy—was a prime example of the dangers.

Needless to say, between T.A.F.T., our personal lives, and side duties (i.e. Runs With Scissors, Love Bites, and helping the police) we were all busy with no time to spare. When Friday rolled around, everyone was exhausted and ready to take a break. My hopes, however, were dashed when I walked in the door and saw Jack sitting on the couch with his head in his hands and coffee cups littering the table in front of him.

"Everything okay?" I set down my purse, kicked off my shoes and rushed over to him.

Jack's head snapped up. "Holy crap! I didn't hear you come in. Was I sleeping?"

I shook my head. "Don't know. I couldn't see your eyes with your face buried in your hands. Is everything okay?" I repeated.

"Yes and no." He rubbed his eyes, reached forward,

and looked into the one upright coffee cup on the table in front of him. He frowned and sighed loudly when he found it was empty.

"Care to expand?" I sat down next to him.

Jack leaned back in the couch. "The good news is Paul made his first move. While 'helping' Sheila with an investment change, he skimmed some money off the top. When she asked him about it, he told her some baloney story about it being a trading fee that was paid to the company who processed the stock."

"And that 'baloney' wasn't true?"

"Yes, and no."

I scrunched up my face. "Seriously?"

Jack grinned when he saw my annoyance. He loved to poke the bear just to get a rise out of me. "The site *does* charge a processing fee, but nowhere near the amount that Paul stated."

"Why would he only skim off the top? I thought his game was taking them for everything they have?" I slumped back in the couch as I tried to understand.

"We think he's testing the waters to not only make sure the account numbers and passwords Sheila has listed are accurate, he's ensuring she really is as clueless about how things work as she's making herself appear."

"Gotcha. I guess that makes sense. If you put a frog in a pot and slowly heat the pot of water to a boil, it won't jump out; you throw it straight into boiling water, it'll hop right out."

"Interesting analogy, but accurate." Jack laughed.

"So, what's the bad news?"

"The way he is playing this makes it like a game of chess. We have to try to think three steps ahead if we're going to be at the right place at the right time to catch him in the act of stealing and provoke him to finish the job. Getting him on wire fraud alone won't keep him behind bars very long." Jack stood up and stretched, raising his hands and lifting toward the ceiling.

"So, too slow to catch on that he's finally stolen everything, then we might not be able to manage his attack on Sheila, and too quick might cause us to tip our hand?"

"Exactly. At any given moment he could make a run for the hills if he feels like he's being watched or set up."

"Well, it's a good thing I'm not running the operation. I suck at chess."

"I remember," he teased, as he moved around the room and collected the empty cups, stacking them one by one into one another. "But don't worry, you have plenty of other talents."

"Do I?" I crossed my legs and raised one eyebrow. "What might they be?"

"Well—" Jack's cell buzzed on the table. "Hold that thought."

He walked over, picked it up, and answered.

"Hello?"

" ... Hold on. Let me go outside; the cell signal inside the house is crap." Jack turned and headed outside.

I got up and ventured into the bedroom to change into something a scant more appropriate for finishing our conversation. Grinning, I slid a silk robe over my selection and belted it at the waste.

Hearing the back door slide open and shut, I made my way back out to the living room. Jack did a double take when he saw me.

"Ready to continue our conversation?"

Jack growled as he gave me an up and down. "Can't. That was Sheila. Paul just surprised her with a getaway to the mountains."

"Crap!" I gasped. "When are they supposed to leave?"

"Tomorrow, mid-morning. Which means whatever he's planning on doing, he might do it in the morning. The woods would be a great place to kill her and dispose of the body."

"So, what are you going to do?"

Jack paced back and forth across the living room. "We're scurrying to set up an operation first thing tomorrow. We'll wait a few blocks away until IT can confirm the money is gone. As soon as we know, we'll stage a call to tip her off. Then, she can confront him."

I moved over to the island and sat on one of the barstools. "What if he isn't planning on stealing the money until after he kills her?"

"It's possible. That's why we've also got a group heading up to the location where they're supposed to be going. We also hid a tracker on both cars, in case he takes a detour."

I felt the blood drain from my face. "But in that scenario, Sheila will be a sitting duck. You can't be right on top of them or he'll figure it out."

"It's a risk we knew was possible. Sheila is a professional and should be able to handle just about anything that comes her way until we can come to her rescue."

"And if she can't?"

"Let's just hope it doesn't come to that."

Chapter Twenty-One

I wanted to go and be a part of saving Sheila, but the only way Jack would let me do that was to go with him to the apartment stakeout. He declared the moving scenario in the mountains was too volatile to risk my being in the way or getting hurt.

So, at the moment, I was sitting in the van having a bit of déjà vu from our previous stakeout. The audio and video surveillance was extremely limited. In order to keep a low profile, they'd only been comfortable installing one wide range camera in a vent in the main room, and then used her open laptop's webcam in the bedroom—deactivating the webcam light so it wouldn't give them away.

Jack sat next to me tapping his foot on the floor while

we waited for confirmation the money had been moved. As of now, we had nothing.

When the phone next to Jack rang, I jumped, startled at the sound even though I prayed it would come. After a quick, quiet conversation Jack hung up and turned to the microphone in front of the monitors.

Jack pressed a button and spoke into the microphone. "We have confirmation that Sheila's accounts have been placed into a pending status." He glanced at the monitors and saw Paul was packed and ready to go. Sheila was moving as slowly as she could without being obvious. "All units get into place. We don't have time to wait for the accounts to clear; we need to stage the phone call in five minutes."

I bit my lip and watched the body cams of the officers who were covering the exits: two at the front, two at the back, and two at the fire escape. They were in full body gear. When the last unit was set, Jack gave me a thumbs up. I had been designated as the person to make the call. Peering down at the script in front of me, I dialed the number. My fingers shook as I hit each one, so much so that I messed up dialing and had to hang up.

Jack reached over and squeezed my knee. "Take a deep breath. You've got this."

I did as instructed, inhaling deeply, holding it for a moment, then exhaling. I picked up the receiver and dialed. I watched on the video screen as Paul—instead of Sheila— moved toward the phone. We'd purposefully turned the sound off in the van, so there was no feedback from the phone against the equipment in her apartment.

"Hello," Paul answered.

"Hello. Can I please speak with Ms. Joy Lovato?" I used Sheila's undercover name and my most formal work tone of voice. I reserved it for when I was trying to seal the deal with a new client.

"May I ask who's calling?"

My heart jumped a bit when I read the script and saw there was no mention of who I was pretending to be. We hadn't considered that Paul might answer her phone. By the flash of emotion that crossed Sheila's face, she hadn't thought so either, though she'd quickly covered up the shock.

"Grace Pemberton." I pulled a name out of thin air.

"With ...?" A bead of sweat trailed down my brow. I didn't know what to say. No one had mentioned the name was of the financial institution he was stealing from. Reaching up, I wiped the sweat away and started to say, "With—"

I watched as Sheila moved forward, grabbed the phone from Paul before I could answer, and glowered at him. I heard her say, "I'm guessing that's for me."

Her tone and expression conveyed just the right amount of annoyance for someone who didn't like just anyone answering their phone without permission.

I sang a silent prayer of thanks! I hadn't wanted to use a different company name because that wouldn't give her the opening she needed to start the "you stole my money" conversation.

"Excuse me?" I said.

"My apologies," Sheila said. "I wasn't speaking to you."

Knowing we didn't need to have a proper conversation, I cut to the chase. Glancing down at the paper, I read aloud, "Is this Ms. Lovato?"

"Yes, it is. How can I help you?"

"This is Grace Pemberton, I'm calling to confirm your accounts have all been placed into a *pending* status. The transfer should be completed shortly."

That wasn't exactly what the script indicated, but again it was written to tell her the money was gone. I thought it best to let her know we were still in somewhat of a "wait and see" moment.

"I'm sorry, what did you say?"

I repeated myself. As I did, I noticed Jack scribbling on a piece of paper.

"Can you tell me who authorized the transactions?"

Jack handed me the paper. I read the words he'd written. "It appears these were completed online using your information. Are you telling me you didn't authorize these transfers?"

I saw Sheila glance at Paul. "Can I get your number and call you right back?"

I listed off a crap phone number, thanked her, and hung up. As soon as the receiver was in the cradle, Jack turned the sound back on in the van.

"Good job," he praised. I exhaled a sigh of relief that I hadn't screwed the pooch before turning to peek at the monitors. We watched as Sheila pivoted around to face Paul.

"Who was that?" Paul asked, as he casually sauntered over to the nearest chair and took a seat.

"That was my bank."

"Is everything okay?" he asked, leaning forward.

Sheila put her hands on her hips. "I don't know. You tell me."

"Tell you what? What exactly did they say?" Paul sat up straight.

"They were calling to confirm that all the transfer requests are in process online and should be completed shortly."

"You transferred all your money? Why? Where?" Paul tilted his head.

"*I* did no such thing." Sheila paced back and forth.

"Well if you didn't do it, who did?"

My eyes were glued on Paul's face. A quick smirk came and went from his lips. Sheila, whose back was turned, wasn't privy to the expression he'd made.

Sheila stopped moving, turned, and faced Paul. "You tell me."

Paul shot up from the couch and took one step forward. "What are you trying to insinuate? That *I* had something to do with moving your money?"

"Don't play stupid with me," She said, her voice eerily calm. She took one step back and widened her stance just a bit. "I know I didn't touch my money. The only other person here who knows my account numbers is you."

"Maybe you've been hacked and your identity was stolen?"

"That seems awfully convenient, doesn't it?" Her eyebrows rose as she loosely placed her arms at her side.

It dawned on me that she was getting into a defensive stance, preparing for whatever Paul was about to do.

"You can't be serious!" Paul growled as he took another step closer. "Is this some sort of game you play?"

"So, you're saying you have no idea what this is about?"

"None."

Sheila took two steps back toward the table that held the phone. "Fine. Then I'll just call them back and tell them to cancel the transfers and lock my accounts."

She took one final step and reached her hand out. Paul jumped forward, grabbed Sheila's arm, and shoved her to the ground.

"I think not," he snarled.

Sheila crab-walked backward until she was as far away as she could get. "So, it was you!"

"Maybe it was, maybe it wasn't. You'll never know." A malicious smile spread over Paul's face as he moved forward.

We had him—I could see it in his eyes. He was like a

beast about to burst free and shred apart his prey. My heart squeezed when I saw how terrified she was; though it might have been exaggerated for his benefit, I could tell at some level it was real. I didn't think any person could stand in front of a killer, knowing they were about to become a victim, and not react in some way even if they knew it was coming.

"What do you mean, I'll never know?" The words came out in a whisper, so soft I think I actually read her lips versus hearing the words over the microphone.

A sinister gleam spread over Paul's features as he took one final step and raised his fist up over his head. "Let me show you!"

I held my breath as I waited for the blow to fall and make contact. The front door burst open, the doorframe splintering with the impact. A single officer raced into the room, gun drawn, the second officer entering a split second later.

"Police! Hands in the air."

"What the fuck!" Jack screamed into the radio. "Who told the rookie to breach?"

The line was silent. Jack flung his radio down onto the table and raced out of the van. Alone, I watched the screen in stunned silence. The officer cuffed Paul and read him his rights. Jack came into view as he burst into the room. The rookie started forward, his arm pulling Paul toward the door.

"Malcolm," Jack said to the other officer, "take him

to the car."

"I got this, boss," the rookie said, as he tried to step past.

Jack grasped the rookie's arm. "Malcolm will take it from here."

The rookie flicked his gaze back and forth between Jack and Officer Malcolm. That's when I saw it: Paul smirked as if he was enjoying the show. Why wasn't he afraid, or at least not smiling?

Glaring, the rookie let Paul go and Malcolm led him out the door. The rookie started to follow.

"I'm not done with you, Abrams." Jack put his hands on his hips. His face was beet red.

The rookie, who I now knew was named Abrams, stopped cold.

"Do you realize what you've just done, son?"

"Yeah," Officer Abrams responded with a grin. "I busted the bastard."

Jack lowered his arms and balled his fists at his side. I saw him take in several deep breaths and flex his hands.

"No. What you did was ruin our operation."

"Ruin it?" Abram's eyebrows shot up. "I just caught the perp before he could hurt Sheila."

Two things I knew at that moment: he was in a shitload of trouble, and he had something—though I didn't know what—for, or with Sheila. Any officer with just professional feelings would have called her Officer Copeland.

"Exactly. You caught him 'before' he did anything."

"What the fuck!" Abrams spat. "You mean we were supposed to let him hit her?"

"That was the whole point of the operation. To catch him *after* he'd actually done something violent. You just allowed his conviction to go from attempted homicide to attempted assault."

"But—"

"But nothing. Detective Copeland was fully aware and on board with the situation she was placing herself in."

"So, she was just supposed to sit there and let him kick the shit out of her?"

"Sheila, since you seem to be on a first name basis with her, is a seasoned undercover detective. She knows how to minimize a blow and how to catch a killer."

Officer Abrams paled as the knowledge of what he'd just done sank in. "Shit."

My heart dropped. I couldn't believe what I'd just heard. All the time and hard work had just been ruined. And here I'd told Jack to give the rookies some slack!

"That's putting it mildly. Rookie or not, this is going to go in your permanent record. You should have known better."

Abram's spine straightened. "You told us to be ready to act fast, to keep her safe."

"What I said was, 'This is going to go down fast. Sheila is relying on us to get her out of this situation alive.'"

"See, you just said to keep her safe."

Jack shook his head and groaned loud enough I heard it. "Alive, not safe. If you're going to continue as an officer, you better learn to listen to what instructions are *actually* being given."

Eyes wide, Abrams just stood there unmoving. It wasn't until Jack moved forward and placed his hand on the rookie's shoulder that he moved, or in all actuality, flinched.

Abrams tilted his head and blinked, but stayed silent.

"We need to get to the station. We'll sort everything out there." Jack removed his hand and moved toward the door.

Officer Abrams' shoulders slumped and he followed, shuffling his feet as he exited. Clearly, the weight of what he'd just done was now bearing down on him.

By the time they made it downstairs, Officer Malcolm had already secured the prisoner and proceeded to the station. The rest of the team filed out, loaded up, and headed to the station.

Chapter Twenty-Two

Because I had been a part of the operation from the start, the captain allowed me to watch through the glass and observe the interrogation. You could cut the tension with a knife as we waited for Jack to show up and begin. Things had gone from bad to worse when we learned the transfer had still been in a pending state when they'd arrested Paul. So, they couldn't even get him on wire fraud, only *attempted* wire fraud.

I was almost certain Paul was aware of the mistake, based on his body language. Although he sat handcuffed to the table, he was casually slouched back into his chair— as best he could—and sported an expression that clearly stated he had not a care in the world. I groaned inwardly at the battle Jack was about to fight.

When Jack walked in, he was bright-eyed and bushy-tailed—which shocked the bejeebers out of me. When I'd last seen him, he'd looked like something the cat had drug in. I guessed some Monster, food, and a quick shower had something to do with the change. The only thing that gave him away was the circles under his eyes.

"Mr. Reynolds, I assume you know why you are here today?" Jack moved over to the table and set down a folder, but he made no move to sit.

"Actually, no I don't." Paul regarded Jack, his head tilted.

"We believe you're responsible for a series of thefts in several states."

"Do you?" His eyebrows shot up. "Why in the world would you think that?"

Jack pulled out the chair and took a seat. "According to your most recent victim, you stole her account numbers and passwords and then attempted to transfer her funds."

"And you have proof of this?"

"We do."

A smug smile stretched across Paul's face. "I'd love to see the proof."

Jack, in reality, had diddly squat. They were still scrambling to figure out who owned the account numbers listed as the transfer-to location. The only thing they'd pinned down was the location: the Cayman Islands. The red tape to get answers from the bank in the Caymans was harder than walking through a minefield blindfolded.

"I'll be happy to show that to you shortly. Right now, however, we'd like to discuss your assault of Ms. Lovato in her apartment."

"Attempted." Paul leaned forward.

"Excuse me?" Jack flicked the corner of the folder and tilted his head.

"You said assault. I never hit her, so it would be attempted assault."

"Oh, I see. So, you're familiar with laws related to assault."

Paul shrugged and arched his lips. "What can I say? I watch a lot of T.V. law shows. Sue me."

"Don't you worry—we plan on doing much more than that." Jack smiled back.

"I guess we'll see how far you get." Paul smirked. "After my lawyer gets here of course."

Everyone on my side let out a collective breath, and one "shit" echoed in the small room. He'd just played his trump card. Now, things got a lot trickier and Jack would be walking a tightrope. The rookie had screwed the operation back, front, and sideways.

"You realize the moment a lawyer steps in here, things get a lot more complicated. It would be easiest on you if you just cooperate and own up to what you've done."

Paul leered. "You'd like that, wouldn't you? You must think I'm really dumb?"

"On the contrary, Paul ... or is it Derek?"

Paul's smirk faltered for the briefest of moments before it returned in all its glory. "I'm sorry—Derek?"

Before Jack could probe any further, the door to the interrogation room burst open and a gentleman in a black suit strode through the room. I guessed him to be in his mid-sixties.

"Excuse me. I believe you are questioning my client without permission." The new man made his way forward and slapped his briefcase onto the table.

"Don't worry, Bernard." Paul smiled. "We were just having a nice chat until you arrived. Weren't we?"

I saw Jack clench and unclench first his jaw, then his fists. "Absolutely."

"Well, then." Bernard bobbed his head. "I would like a few minutes alone with my client if you wish to continue to speak with him."

"No. I believe we're all done for the time being. You can go ahead and go with him to booking." Jack moved to the still-open door and waved in an officer. "Just follow Officer Blake."

"That won't be necessary. I will be paying whatever bail is set."

"Oh, dear." Jack rubbed his chin. "Did you not realize the courts were closed for the weekend? Judge Hamilton won't be free until Monday to hear Mr. Murphy's case."

"That is unacceptable. I want to speak with your captain right this minute."

Jack shrugged. "He's out until Monday as well. I'm the

senior officer on duty. So, I apologize, but you'll just have to come back Monday morning, bright and early."

Bernard yanked his briefcase off the desk and shot daggers at Jack with his glare. "Paul, let's go with the officer."

Hamilton moved forward, uncuffed Paul from the table on the bar, and started to escort him and Bernard out the door. On the way out, however, Paul bumped into Jack and whispered something to him that I don't think anyone else could make out.

Jack's shoulders tensed as he sidestepped and let the officer remove the men from the room.

"I'll be having a word with both your superior and the judge on Monday about your conduct, Detective," Bernard said over his shoulder after he crossed the threshold.

"Be my guest," Jack said. When the doorway was clear, Jack turned and shot a look toward the mirror. The expression on his face was not good.

***

I was ushered into Jack's office while he had a meeting with his people. The clock indicated it was just after two, but it felt like this day had been going on forever. The growl of my stomach reminded me that I hadn't eaten since first thing this morning. Not knowing when Jack would be done, I went out to the vending machine and purchased a snack and drink.

The only snack option that was the least bit appealing was a bag of trail mix. I opened the bag, poured some into my palm, then tossed it into my mouth. Normally I enjoyed when the peanuts met the chocolate, however, at the current moment, it all tasted like cardboard.

I had no idea what Jack could do to save the situation. From what I saw, they had squat. While they might be able to try him on attempted assault in the near future, that still wouldn't warrant much bail money. At least they had until Monday to figure something out and potentially tie Paul to the wire transaction. With that, they might stand a fighting chance. I crossed my fingers they would find something—anything—to get and keep this man behind bars.

After finishing off my pseudo-meal, I tossed the items in the trash and checked my voicemail. At least there weren't any fires at work to take care of. All was going surprisingly well on that front. As I hung up my phone, the door opened. When Jack walked in, I could tell the Monster rush had worn off; he looked like crap.

I stood and pulled him into a hug. We stood like that for several minutes, soaking in the silence and the comfort of one another. Finally he pulled back, moved to his chair, and sank down into it.

"That bad, huh?"

"Worse." Jack sat back, closed his eyes, and brushed his hands through his hair.

I sat quietly, hands folded in my lap as I waited for him to collect himself, though I was biting at the bit to ask him what Paul had whispered to him on the way out.

When he opened his eyes, he gave me a once-over and grinned. "You want to know what he said, don't you?

"How—"

"When do you ever sit still and quiet unless you want something?"

"That's not true." I sat back, crossed my arms, and huffed.

Jack's laugh lit up his whole face and helped to remove some of the darkness that had clung to him when he'd entered. "Sure … if you say so."

We sat in silence; the longer the silence the bigger the smile on Jack's face and the deeper my scowl. "Fine! You're right. I want to know what he told you."

Jack cleared his throat and tried to wipe the smile off his face—unsuccessfully, I might add. He leaned forward and his face darkened, the previous moments of joy gone. He whispered, "Did you truly believe it would be that easy?"

I sucked in a breath. "Wow. That takes balls!"

"Yep." Jack clenched and unclenched his fits several times while he attempted to keep his blood pressure from rising again. "But then again, he's got us by ours. The Rookie's mistake is costing us big time."

"Did you get the information from the bank yet?" I reached forward and placed my hands over his and rubbed my thumb over them. After a few moments, I felt his hands relax.

Jack leaned forward, took my hand to his lips, and laid a gentle kiss. "Not yet. But we've got our best people on it."

"I'll keep my fingers crossed. We both know the son-of-a-bitch is guilty. We can't let him go."

"Agreed. I've got a couple more things to finish up here. Why don't you go home and get some rest, then we can go out for dinner?"

"Manga's?"

Jack licked his lips. "Manga's sounds perfect!"

Chapter Twenty-Three

Sunday afternoon, I parked my car and walked into the station. When I got to the front desk, I was informed that Jack was in the back in evidence lock-up. I was buzzed through and pointed in the appropriate direction.

There was no one manning the desk at the evidence locker so I hollered, "Hello? Jack, are you in here?"

Footsteps echoed in the other room, growing heavier as they made their way to me. As the footsteps rounded the corner, I saw they belonged not to Jack but to another officer.

"Hey, Callie," Officer Donolie said. "Jack's not here. He went back to Paul's apartment to do one more sweep."

"Darn it. I was hoping to catch him before he went

anywhere else. I assumed both he and Sheila would be here."

"Nope, sorry. Sheila has the day off. She's recovering from having been bait for the case. Did you try Jack's cell? He always answers."

"I did. He didn't answer. I just assumed he was busy," I said. "Let me try him again."

I grabbed out my cell phone as Donolie watched. I punched redial and waited. It rang three times before once again going to voicemail.

"Jack, it's Callie. Call me when you get this." I hung up and put my phone back in my purse.

"No luck?"

I shook my head. "Nope. Still nothing."

"There's probably no signal. Sometimes apartment complexes can be shoddy on cell service, with all the interference from everyone's devices."

"You're probably right," I said. "Is there any way you could give me the address, so I can go over and try to catch him there?"

"Come on back and I'll see if I can't find the address."

Reaching over he pushed a button. A buzz sounded to my right as the cage door unlocked. I pushed it open and moved inside. I followed him into the room and around the corner.

"What's all this?" I asked, waving my arm in an arc to indicate the mass of evidence envelopes on top of a long table.

"This is all of the evidence connected to Mr. Reynolds—from all the different counties. I'm getting ready to comb through it again and see if we missed anything."

"And they said you guys never get to have any fun." I chuckled.

"Yeah, fun times," he guffawed. He picked up a file folder off the table and flipped it open. When he saw what he needed, he grabbed a pen and notepad out of his chest pocket and wrote something down before handing the paper to me.

"Here's the address he should be at."

"Thanks." I took the paper. As I moved to leave, a colorful object in one of the evidence bags caught my attention. "What's that?"

"What?" His gaze followed mine.

"That." I pointed.

He followed my aim and picked up the bag. Holding it up, he turned it this way and that. "What the heck is this?"

He lifted the object toward me so I could get a close-up. My chest tightened as I stared at it. Not because I didn't know what it was, but because I *did* know.

I remembered commenting on the unique design and replayed in my mind when Pepper had leaned forward and extended her hand so I could get a better look at her fingernail. The flashback caused one very large looming question to form in my mind ... Why in the world would that be here, in this crime scene evidence, no less?

"You okay?" Donolie's forehead wrinkled. "Do you know what this is?"

"Yes, to both."

"What is it?" He lifted it closer and scrutinized the object further.

"It's an acrylic fingernail, or at least it *was* an acrylic nail." I viewed the small jagged chunk of what once was a flame design decorated nail.

"Huh. Must have belonged to one of the vics." He shrugged as he set the bagged item back down on the table.

"No, I'm certain it's not."

I started pacing back and forth as I tried to figure out why that would be here, of all places. The butterflies in my stomach intensified.

I recalled what he'd whispered to Jack at the end of the interrogation and how he'd seemed almost chipper— like the cat that had caught the canary—as if he knew something the police didn't. Jack had assumed it had to do with the fact they could only charge Paul with attempted assault, not attempted murder, since all he had done was raise his hand to hit Sheila.

Officer Donolie's voice interrupted my thoughts. "How could you possibly know this isn't one of the previous victims?"

I stopped pacing and turned back to the officer. "I've seen that fingernail on someone just recently, and she was very much alive. So, I know it doesn't belong to a victim.

Besides, that evidence bag has yesterday's date on it and it says 'apartment.'"

"Well, I'm sure fake nails are a dime a dozen."

"In most cases yes, but not that one ... it's custom."

Donolie grabbed the baggie again and squinted at it one more time. "How do you know it's custom?"

"Because the woman who had it on her finger told me so. She explained it was a custom design she created and did herself."

"Well, what the heck would that be doing in Mr. Reynold's apartment?"

"I have no idea, but we need to get a hold of Jack right away. Sheila might not have been his only victim!"

Donolie raced to the desk at the front of the evidence locker and called dispatch. He told them to have the nearest officer find Jack and have him call into the line where they were.

While we were waiting for the return the call, I phoned Becky at the office.

"Becky, it's Callie. I need you to do me a favor."

" ... You should have recently received an email from the client that came in the other day—Pepper. Can you check to see if you have it?"

" ... Ok, terrific. I need you to open it and read over her application, specifically her likes/hobbies to see if she noted hockey."

I knew it wasn't the full application—because Pepper had explained she couldn't afford it yet—but she'd sent us her basic profile, so we'd have it loaded in our system when she was ready to hit the go button.

" … Darn. Ok, now check to see if she showed any record of alimony."

" … Bingo! Can you tell me her phone number?"

" … Thanks, Becky. You're a doll."

I quickly hung up and dialed Pepper's number. Straight to voicemail. That wasn't good!

Just as I hung up, the phone at the desk rang. Donolie picked it up.

"Donolie," he said.

" … Yes. We called you."

" … I'm here with Callie, we have a development."

" … She was here to talk to you, but that's not the point." Donolie rubbed his hand through his hair and loudly exhaled. "The point is, she saw something in the crime scene evidence that leads her to believe Sheila wasn't the only intended victim."

I waved at Donolie to get his attention.

" … Hold on, Jack." He moved his gaze to me.

"Tell Jack the—"

Donolie reached the phone out to me. "Here. Just tell him yourself. It'll go quicker."

I took the phone from him. "Jack. Paul might've had a reason for being coy. I think he might have one of my potential clients, Pepper Walsh, stashed somewhere. Her profile shows she was married right out of high school, but it didn't last and she is receiving alimony."

" ... No. She didn't specifically list hockey, but Becky noted Pepper had run out of room on the form for that topic. So, it is still potentially possible that was something she enjoyed."

I shifted from foot to foot as the line went silent except for Jack's breathing. I knew Jack was running all the information I'd told him through his mind and was planning the next course of action.

" ... Okay." I turned to Donolie. "He wants to talk to you again."

He took the phone. " ... I'll get right on it. Sure, no problem. I'll let her know."

He hung up the phone, only to pick it right back up. He asked whoever was on the other end to get Pepper's address and to send it over to him and Jack immediately.

When he hung up, he turned to me. "Jack told me to take you to meet him at Pepper's. He wants you to scope out her apartment and see if anything stands out to you as odd."

I nodded and without further questions, followed Donolie out to his squad car. My stomach filled with knots as I prayed that Pepper wasn't in danger.

Chapter Twenty-Four

Donolie had run his lights and sirens, so we arrived at Pepper's place in no time at all. Jack was waiting outside her front door.

"Have you checked inside yet?" Donolie asked Jack.

"No. I just got here." Jack's gaze fell down to mine. "Stay here. We'll be right back."

I moved to the side and let Donolie past. Jack knocked on the door and waited. After the second try with no answer, he used a set of lockpicks to open the deadbolt.

Holding my breath, I leaned against the wall. No noise came from the apartment except for footsteps. Several moments later, Jack's head popped back out the door.

"No one's here." He motioned me inside. "Take a

look around and see if you can find anything off."

Stepping forward, I walked in and carefully scoped out the surroundings. The apartment was nothing special. The entryway led into a small living room/dining room combo; to the left was a small galley-style kitchen which ended in a washer/dryer room hidden by sliding doors.

Looking in the kitchen, I saw the sink was empty and the counters were clear of dishes. A dish rack sat next to the sink and held two coffee cups, two plates, and two forks. Seeing the cups, I realized the aroma of coffee lingered in the air. *Was it my imagination?*

I made my way over to the sink and picked up one of the cups. A drop of water dripped on my hand when I turned it over to look inside.

"I think someone was just here," I declared loudly, so Jack could hear me in the other room. "There are coffee cups that are still wet in the drying rack and I smell coffee."

"Did you say coffee cups, plural?"

"Yep." I moved out of the kitchen to the living room. Fear making all my senses hyper-alert, I scanned over every object in detail in hopes of seeing a clue that might lead us to Pepper. Lucky for us, Pepper kept a very tidy space, so searching was easy.

The room was small and held few objects: a couch, coffee table, fake plant, an entertainment center with a television, and a corner table. As I finished surveying the room, my gaze landed on the small corner table stacked with magazines. I noticed an item peeking out from the bottom of the stack that I recognized. Proceeding forward, I reached out and slid the T.A.F.T. brochure out of the stack. Had I not been intimately familiar with the object, I probably wouldn't have noticed it.

"Find anything else interesting?" Donolie asked, as he rounded the corner into the room.

"Nope." I laid the flyer back down onto the table. "Let me take a look at the bedroom and bathroom."

I continued to the right and into the bedroom. The room was painted a powder-blue and contained a queen-sized bed, two narrow nightstands, a tower dresser, and a TV stand.

I took care to walk around the entire room and look both at eye level and on the ground for anything amiss. Seeing nothing, I squatted down and took stock of any items under each piece of furniture. Finding nothing, I moved to the bathroom.

On the countertop in the bathroom was a small caddy which was open to show several bottles of polish; all the colors of Pepper's current fingernail design were present. I noticed there was also a small box of Band-Aids sitting on the countertop.

Jack appeared in the doorway. "Do you see any items that could be helpful?"

"No, not really." I shook my head. "Nothing seems odd to me besides the two coffee cups."

"What the hell!" screeched a female voice from the other room.

Jack and I both hightailed it into the living room in time to see Donolie, hands raised, standing still while Pepper aimed a can of pepper spray at his face—the irony of that was not lost on me.

"It's okay, ma'am. I'm officer Donolie." *Thank God he was in uniform.*

Pepper moved her gaze to both of us as we entered. She did a double-take when she saw me.

"It's okay, Pepper. We're here to help you," I said.

Pepper's arm faltered and lowered slightly as she stared dumbfounded at me. "Help me?"

Donolie moved and Pepper jerked her canister back up. "Someone had better start explaining right now!"

I raised my hands and moved forward. I assumed I was the best person to de-escalate the situation since Pepper knew me.

"Pepper, we're here because we thought you might be in danger. We only came in unannounced to ensure you were okay. When we didn't find you, we started looking for clues."

She tilted her head and her brows scrunched together. "In danger? Why would you presume I'm in danger?"

"Long story short, I found one of your fingernails at a crime scene. We weren't certain what had happened to the rest of you."

"You mean this?" She held up her finger, which was adorned with an emoji Band-Aid. "I broke this at my boyfriend's apartment."

Jack took a step toward Pepper, arm outstretched. "You can put the pepper spray down, Ms. Walsh."

She blinked a moment before looking at her hand. "Oh, sorry. I forgot about that." She lowered her hand.

"No problem. We do apologize for the unexpected intrusion. Would you mind telling me your boyfriend's name?"

"Kyle Murphy."

Jack and I looked at each other, the same expression on both of our faces. Then a light bulb went off, and I reached into my back pocket. I lifted the phone and it unlocked. Quickly, I went into my camera and scrolled through my photos in search of the one the tech team had sent me at Love Bites.

I turned my phone around, stepped closer to Pepper, and asked, "Is this Kyle?"

Pepper quickly viewed the photo, a smile lighting her face. "Yep, that's him." The smile quickly faded. "Wait, did you say crime scene? Kyle's apartment is a crime scene?" She paled.

I looked at Jack. I wasn't about to step on that landmine. I didn't have the proper training to break that kind of news. Pepper glanced from me to Jack when she saw I wasn't going to answer.

"I'm afraid so—"

Pepper swooned on her feet; Donolie rushed forward and grabbed her before she fell. He gently led her to the couch and helped her sit. She put her head in her hands and took several deep breaths. Jack stood silently as he waited for her to recover. When she looked back up, there were tears glistening in her eyes.

"Is he okay?"

Jack and Donolie made eye contact before Jack turned his gaze to her. "He's okay, but in police custody."

"Police custody." Pepper's spine straightened.

"Yes. He was arrested last night at—"

Pepper raised her hand into the air. "Hold up. Last night? There's no way you arrested him last night."

"I know this is hard for you to hear, but—"

"No." She lowered her hand and cemented her gaze on Jack. "I'm telling you that's impossible. Kyle was here all night and this morning. In fact, he just left right before my run. He mentioned he had some loose ends to tie up today."

Loose ends? I dropped into the closest chair—no need to give the boys someone else to worry about fainting—my mouth going dry.

Jack reached his hand out to me. "Callie, give her your phone again, please."

I reached into my back pocket, turned it on, and handed it to her.

"Please look again very carefully," Jack instructed. "Are you certain *this* is Kyle?"

This time, Pepper took the phone and brought it closer instead of just looking at it from afar. She shook her head. "Yes. That's Kyle."

When the three of us didn't respond, Pepper stood. "Hold on a second." She walked over to the door, bent down, and picked up a set of keys and a phone from the floor. She must've dropped the items when she'd entered and found Officer Donolie.

She tossed the keys on the entry table before making her way back to us. She lifted the phone and swiped her finger over the screen. Within a few moments, she turned the phone around. We all craned our necks to get a peek. On the screen was Paul, a.k.a. Derek, a.k.a. Kyle, asleep on the couch.

"He doesn't know I took this. He hates having his picture taken, but he just looked so darn cute I couldn't help myself." Her eyes sparkled as she looked at the screen. It was apparent she cared for him.

There was no doubt the picture was of Paul. But how was that possible?

"Do you have anything he's touched recently that might have a fingerprint?" Jack asked.

Pepper tapped her finger on her chin for a moment before her eyebrows rose. "There's a glass on the bathroom counter that he uses to rinse after he brushes his teeth."

Jack moved toward the bathroom, and for some reason Donolie headed outside. I, though, turned my attention to Pepper. "When did you meet Pa—" I stopped myself. "I mean Kyle?"

Pepper blushed. "We met about a week ago. I was at

the grocery store, in the produce section, and he asked me if I knew how to tell if a melon was ripe."

Puzzle pieces clicked into place in my mind. A week ago would've been right after we'd shipped Vanessa off to the Caribbean, and his grocery store produce pickup was the same one he'd used on her. Well, at least his MO was consistent. He sure hadn't wasted any time moving on to his next mark. But if Paul was in jail and Kyle was just here, who was *he*?

Just as Jack walked back into the room, Donolie returned, carrying a black toolbox type case. He made his way over to Jack, set the box down, and opened the lid.

First, he pulled out a small container and a brush, then he removed a palm-sized black device. He opened the container and swirled the brush around; powder floated into the air. Jack handed him the glass. Donolie gently spun the brush back and forth, dusting the glass with powder as he rotated it three-sixty. Once the glass was covered, he held it up to the light, turning it this way and that. Deep, fine lines gathered between his eyes as he scrutinized the glass.

He stopped, lowered the glass, raised the black device, punched a button, and then ran it slowly down a section of the glass. That's when it dawned on me the device was some sort of hand-held scanner. A boisterous buzz sounded and he cursed under his breath. He tried again. After the third attempt, the buzz changed into a chirpy ding.

He set the glass down and stared at the machine. We all sat silently waiting for the device to do its thing. The tick-tock sound of a clock situated in the kitchen filled the air. When the machine finally made another noise, I let out a breath I didn't know I'd been holding.

Donolie did a double take of the screen before handing the device to Jack.

"What is it?" I asked, fear running down my spine like tiny ants making their way into their hill.

Jack and Donolie started for the door. "You stay here with Pepper," Jack snapped. "Lock the doors and if Kyle, Derek, or Paul shows up here, do *not* let him in. Call it in to the station."

"What's wrong?!" I followed them out the door.

Jack, without turning, said over his shoulder, "I fear he's going after Sheila."

I didn't understand all of what had just happened, but I knew it was not the time for more questions. I walked back inside the apartment, closed the door, and locked it. I leaned against the closed door and slid down to the ground. *Please, God. Let them get there in time!*

***

I wasn't sure who paced more while we waited for someone to return—me or Pepper. It was going on two hours since Jack had left. I longed to fill Pepper in on all that she'd missed, but I didn't want to mess up anything in the case by divulging too much.

When I was unable to handle the tense silence any longer, I glanced around the room and looked for a hint of something we could talk about. I walked over to the entertainment center and picked up a photograph that was placed beside the television. It held the portrait of an older couple, the man sporting red hair to match Pepper's, though his was paler and peppered with white.

"Those are my parents," Pepper said from behind me.

"Your dad's hair was a dead giveaway!" I smiled, put the picture down, and turned.

"Yep. We love the red hair in my family."

"Do you have any siblings? I don't recall any on your profile."

"No. I think that's why Dad loved Sawyer so much. He was the son he never had."

"I take it Sawyer is your ex?"

"The one and only." Pepper stopped pacing, moved over to the couch, and took a seat. "I really thought I'd gotten lucky and had found my soulmate."

I followed her lead and sat down on the couch. "What happened?"

"The real world happened."

I tilted my head, my brows pinching together. "Real world?"

Pepper slumped back against the cushions. "When you're in a small town, you pretty much know everyone. When you get the cream of the crop from what is available, you think you've won the lottery. But once you leave the small town and realize there is so much more out there ... "

Belmont was a small-ish town, so I had a general idea what Pepper meant. "That makes sense."

"We both loved each other, but once we saw how much more there was to explore, we knew it was best to go our separate ways for a short while. I mean, we weren't even twenty when we got married."

"I can't even imagine how tough a choice that must've been."

"Yeah. Deep down I thought we'd end up back together, that we were "meant to be", but it never happened. Sawyer fell in with a rich, pretty, party crowd and never looked back."

I watched as Pepper blinked back tears. I reached out and patted her knee. "I'm sorry it ended that way."

It was in the moment of silence that transpired that Pepper's phone rang. Normally, it wouldn't have startled either of us. However, with the underlying tension, we both jumped; Pepper let out a tiny squeal.

She scrambled over to the countertop and grabbed it. "Hello?"

The tension in her faced evaporated after a moment. "Thanks for the information, Mrs. Algorn. I'll come down and get it."

Pepper touched the screen and laid the phone back down on the table.

"I'm guessing that wasn't related to Kyle?"

"No. Sorry. That was my downstairs neighbor. She got some of my mail by accident and just wanted to let me know."

I let out a sigh and watched as Pepper headed toward the door. "You're not going right now to get that, are you?"

Pepper unlocked the door and turned the knob. "Sure, why not? It's only two flights down. I highly doubt anyone is going to sneak up on me in the time it takes to—"

A scream ripped out of Pepper's mouth as she opened the door and a form moved into the doorway. Pepper scrambled backward into the apartment.

Without realizing it, I had grabbed up the candlestick from the table beside me and headed toward the door and the unknown person.

I'd taken two steps when recognition struck. Officer Kata—the surfer-haired man I'd met at the front desk in the police station—stood at the door, gun raised and pointed. The expression on his face, along with the pointed weapon, told me he was as shocked about what had transpired as we had been.

Officer Kata split his gaze back and forth between me and Pepper. As the tension released from his frame and expression, he returned his weapon to the holster. "Sorry about that."

I nodded and watched as he took a step forward, turning his full attention to me. "Ms. Bloom, it's Officer Kata. We met the other day at the front desk when you came in looking for Detective Brown."

I lowered the candlestick, stepped back, and motioned him inside. "I remember."

"Detective Brown asked me to come get you and Ms. Walsh and escort you to the station."

My pulse jumped in my throat as I recalled why he was here to collect us. "What happened? Is Sheila all right?"

"I'm sorry, Ms. Bloom. I can't disclose that information at this time. Detective Brown will fill you in when we get there."

I swallowed hard and nodded. When I turned back, I saw Pepper was already gathering her belongings. I grabbed my purse and we followed the officer to his squad car. My stomach was in knots as I waited to hear what had become of Sheila.

***

The station was more somber than usual when we arrived. That was not a good sign. Officer Kata signed us in at the front desk before escorting Pepper to his station desk, and me to Jack's office. They needed to get a statement from Pepper.

I sat, pulled out my phone, and scrolled through my emails. I'd already done this numerous times while at Pepper's, but I had to keep busy doing something. After several minutes passed, I couldn't take it any longer, so I stood and paced. My heel ached a bit from a blister that was forming from all my pacing to and fro. I welcomed the pain, as it kept me from running various scenarios through my mind of what might have become of Sheila.

Finally, after what seemed like an eternity, Jack entered. He looked awful. His face was pale, his skin drawn, and brown circles surrounded his eyes. He rushed over to me and swallowed me whole into a hug.

"Jack, I can't breathe," I squeaked.

Jack released me and took a step back. "Sorry. I didn't mean to—"

"It's fine." I pulled him back in for a less boa-like hug. He rested his chin on my head and let out several shaky breaths.

After a moment, I moved back. "Can I assume from your reaction that things didn't go well?"

"Yes, and no."

I shot daggers at Jack as he made his way around the desk and sat down. I opened my mouth, but Jack raised his arm and stopped me. He pointed to the chair. I sat.

"When we arrived, we heard multiple shots fired. We found both Kyle and Sheila down on the ground in her apartment, with gunshot wounds."

My hand flew to my chest. "Dear God. Is she okay?"

"She's in intensive care."

My arm lowered back to my lap. "And Kyle?"

"Dead. We don't know exactly what transpired other than he took a double-tap shot to center mass, dying instantly. Kyle also got off two shots, but only one hit

Sheila in the chest. The other went wide."

"What does the doctor say?" I sat forward in my chair.

"They are cautiously optimistic. It doesn't appear any major organs were hit—he missed by millimeters—but she's still lost a lot of blood. It was only because we got there when we did that she's still alive and didn't bleed out."

I let out a sigh. At least she stood a fighting chance. I raised my gaze to Jack. "I'm glad you got there in time. I still don't get it though. How could Paul be in two places at once? Or did he get bailed out last night?"

"Because there are two of him."

"What?" I tilted my head.

"Sorry. Let me be more precise. He has a twin."

"Twin!" I shot up from my seat and started pacing. Jack leaned back in his chair. "How did we not know this?"

"It's complicated and I'm exhausted. How about we take this discussion home where I can get a shower, some food, and some rest."

I stopped pacing and turned to him, worry lines creasing my forehead. "Of course. I should have realized … instead of assaulting you with questions."

He stopped, moved forward, and gave me a gentle kiss. "I get it. There are a lot of holes. Just let me catch my breath a bit and I'll give you all the details."

I shook my head, watched him gather his items, and we headed home.

Chapter Twenty-Five

Jack had eaten a bit, showered, and then laid down for a nap. The nap had gone from "quick" to "overnight". I was okay with it. Jack needed sleep more than I needed answers.

When he finally awoke, got a cup of coffee, and had eaten, we moved to the couch for him to fill me in.

"Remind me where I left off?" he said.

"Twins," I said, as I settled into the couch, folding my legs underneath me and hugging a couch pillow like it was story time. "The last thing I knew was you all looked at the fingerprint scanner and left, then at the station you mentioned twins."

"Gotcha. When we scanned the fingerprint against

Paul's, it came back as no match. So, on a whim I tried it against the partial we'd recovered from the crime scene. When it was a match, it dawned on me we might be looking for two people, i.e. twins."

"Oh my gosh! I guess that makes sense. But how come he didn't show up with a fingerprint in the system if Paul had one? And how did you not know that Paul was a twin?"

"We never felt the need to check birth records on Paul because his fingerprint and identity were in the system. It wasn't until last night that we dug that far back."

"What did it say?"

"That's where it got tricky. We had to have a judge unseal the records."

"Unseal? Why would his birth records be sealed?" My brows furrowed.

"Because it was a closed adoption. The twins were both given up after birth and each was placed with a different family."

I laid the pillow on my lap. "That still doesn't explain why Derek ... or Kyle ... or whoever he is, doesn't exist."

"We don't have all the pieces yet, but it appears they found each other somewhere along the way and decided to live one life. The only twin that ever registered a fingerprint was Paul. We found a duplicate of his driver's license in his brother, Kyle's, possession."

"So, was Derek Paul or Kyle?"

"We don't know for certain. Since we didn't acquire

any fingerprints from him, we never confirmed his identity."

"I thought twins shared fingerprints?"

Jack stood, trekked to the kitchen, and got a refill of coffee. "Nope. Fingerprints are not formed from genetics. So, every individual has a unique set."

"So, we don't have anything solid to tie Paul to the crime scenes."

Jack turned from the counter, his coffee cup steaming. "Not yet. When we went over Kyle's body, we found a set of keys to a storage unit. We were able to locate the unit and hit the jackpot. There were pictures of all of the victims, plus trophies. One of the trophies had two different types of blood on it. We're hoping at least one of the samples might belong to Paul."

I unfolded my legs and leaned forward. "But isn't blood DNA identical?"

"Twins do share the same genetic code."

"So, we're screwed there as well? We can't confirm if it was Paul or Kyle who killed the girls?" My shoulders slumped.

Jack took a drink, swallowed, then answered. "Once upon a time, it would've been extremely difficult to tell them apart. However, now scientists can sequence the entire genome and look for subtle, rare differences."

"That's good, right? It means you can tell which twin committed that murder?"

"Yes and—"

"Say it and die." I glared.

He just grinned lazily, sat down, and continued. "It can be done, but it is very expensive and takes several weeks to accomplish."

I stood and paced, wincing when the pain in my heel twinged, reminding me I had done this a few too many times yesterday. I plopped back down.

"How will you tie the grand larceny to Paul if there's no DNA, just account numbers?"

Jack clenched his jaw. "We can't specifically, unless we find something on his computer or personal electronics that points back to him. Even then, he could say his brother used his computer and did it without his knowledge."

"And since his brother is dead, there isn't anyone to dispute the claim."

"Correct."

I shook my head and rubbed my temples. "This just keeps getting better and better."

Jack took a sip of coffee. "The good news is, one killer is dead, and there were enough financial transactions between the three cases that we might get lucky enough to tie it solidly to Paul."

"And if you don't?"

"We'll get him on attempted assault and he'll get a record. He will no longer be a ghost. If he ever tries the stunt again, the chances of him getting caught go up exponentially."

"I guess if we're lucky, Paul will only have been interested in the money and Kyle interested in killing. So, Paul might steal, but not kill."

"That's a good point. We're going to have our profiler put together something based on Pepper's information and see if we can figure anything out."

"How is Pepper?" I asked, as I stood and took Jack's now empty coffee cup to the sink and rinsed it out.

"I'm not sure. All I know is that the interview went smoothly."

"Would it be okay if I go check on her?"

Jack stood and made his way over to me. "I don't see why not. Just try to limit your conversation to what she already knows. We don't need any of the details I just told you going public just yet."

"Got it."

Jack's cell phone buzzed on the counter.

"Hello … "

"Hang on a sec, let me go outside." He groaned.

We really need to get better cell service if we are going to stay in this house!

As I finished loading the dishwasher with the breakfast dishes, Jack returned.

"That was the hospital. Sheila's awake and alert. I need to go take a statement. Want to go with me?"

I bumped the dishwasher door shut with my hip and dried my hands on the towel hanging by the sink. "As long as it's allowed, sure."

We quickly got ready and headed to the hospital.

***

Sheila was as pale white as the bedsheets she lay upon, her dark chestnut-brown hair a stark contrast against it. Gauze bandages on her right side peeked out from under her blue hospital gown.

The room was a dirty, butter-cream yellow. Machines of all sorts and shapes stood around the head of her bed. Several drip lines connected to those machines ran into an I.V. placed into her arm. On the other hand lay the oxygen monitor. I watched the heart rate monitor as each beat registered with a line, the rhythm soothing in its consistency.

She turned her head and blinked several times when we entered the room. After a moment, a weak smile appeared on her face.

"Jack! Callie! How are you?"

I moved forward and gently took her hand in mine. "I believe the more appropriate question is, 'How are you?'"

"I'm as well as can be expected, given the circumstances."

Letting go of her hand, I moved over and occupied the guest chair, so Jack could take my place beside the bed.

"Are you up to giving a statement?" Jack asked. "If you're not, we can come back."

Sheila shook her head. "Now's as good a time as any.

Not like I've got any place to go at the moment."

Jack pulled the only remaining seat—a doctor's rolling stool—toward him. I started to jump up, but Jack waved me down. "The stool's fine."

I acquiesced and kept my seat. Jack took his trusty notepad and pen from the inside pocket of his jacket.

"Can you tell us what you remember?" Jack asked softly.

Sheila closed her eyes for a moment before answering. "I'd just come home from the shooting range, where I'd gone to decompress from the day before. Right after I finished tossing my bag on the side table and kicking my shoes off, the doorbell rang."

Jack jotted down notes when Sheila paused. She pivoted her head and gazed out the window. "I stepped forward to the door and looked out the peep-hole. I saw a pizza delivery guy, head bent, looking down at a slip of paper lying on top of the pizza box."

"You didn't wait to see his face before you opened the door?" Jack's brows knit together.

Sheila swiveled her attention back to Jack. "It wasn't unusual that the pizza guy was at my door. My next-door neighbors are an elderly couple with very thick accents. It isn't uncommon the delivery place hears 34B instead of 34C."

"I see." Jack made some more notes on his paper. "What happened when you opened the door?"

"Before he even looked up, I started to tell him he had

the wrong apartment. But before I got the words out, he lifted his head and I saw who it was. I remember taking a step backward as I tried to make sense of it ...

"Before I could, he pushed his way in, sending me down to the ground. I froze and flashed back to the night before."

Sheila paled even more—though I didn't know how that was possible—and her pulse and blood pressure increased. I wanted to move forward and comfort her, but I didn't want to break the trance she was in, just in case what she was seeing would be lost.

"What did you do?" Jack's tone was so soft I almost didn't hear it.

"Nothing. I laid back frozen and watched as he tossed the box to the side and pulled a gun out of his jacket. It was only after I saw the gun that I moved backward. I recall saying one word—*how?*

"What did he say?" Jack flipped the page in his notebook.

"He didn't. He just laughed. But his laugh was ... wrong somehow. I'd heard him laugh before, but it hadn't sounded like that. I couldn't put a finger on what was off; I just knew it wasn't right. That snapped me out of my trance enough to register two things. First, that I was in danger. Second, and most importantly, my hand was on my purse. I must've knocked it off the table when he'd shoved me backward."

"What was important about your purse?" Jack asked,

as he tapped his pen against his lips. I found myself leaning forward, waiting for the answer.

"My gun. I hadn't had time to take it out and lock it in my safe. I knew I needed to distract him in order to get in and get it, so I started talking. I asked him if he'd come to admit he'd stolen my money."

"That must've confused him."

"Just for a moment, but then he cackled and told me to cut the crap. He knew I was a cop and that we'd set up his brother.

"Then it was my turn to be stunned. But it also helped to clear up the confusion in my mind about what was off. I knew the only way to get him to shift his gaze was to put it on something else. He wasn't close enough for me to kick, so I did all I could do. I flicked my gaze behind him and pretended a look of hope as if someone was walking by behind him." Sheila flicked her gaze to me, then to Jack.

"I'm guessing from the outcome it worked?" Jack stopped writing and gave his full attention to her.

"I couldn't believe it, but it did. He glanced behind him just long enough for me to grab my gun out and aim. I wasn't quick enough to get a shot off before he turned around and returned fire. My saving grace was my first shot caused his arm to jump just enough for his second shot to go high. Mine, however, because my arm was stabilized on the ground, did not."

"That was still one hell of a move, to pull your gun out and shoot with such precision in the blink of an eye,"

I blurted, unable to stop myself.

Sheila flicked her gaze to me and blushed.

"Sheila started out with the armed forces as a close combat specialist. If anyone could pull that wild west move, it's her."

"Just call me Wild Bill." Sheila chuckled before she grabbed her chest and flinched in pain. "Dear Lord, that hurts."

The door burst open and in rushed a nurse. Both Jack and I froze when we realized who it was. Judy Moore, a.k.a. Nurse Rachet. She'd taken care of me after one of my incidents the previous year. She was not a lady to mess with.

Her eyebrows rose and her lips flattened into a straight line when her gaze found Jack. "You again!"

Jack tipped an imaginary hat at Judy. "Ma'am."

"I see you're bothering my patients again?"

"Just trying to do my job."

Judy put one hand on her hip and used the other to point a finger at Jack. "Well, you'd best do it more carefully. If her blood pressure goes up again, I *will* kick you out of here."

Jack crossed his heart with his finger. "I will do my best. We're almost done here anyway."

She blushed just a bit at the smile Jack tossed her way—he was known for making the ladies swoon. She narrowed her eyes and looked at each of us individually, did a one-eighty, and marched out the door, her shoes squeaking on the tile floor as she went.

"I take it you two know her?"

We both cracked up in unison.

Chapter Twenty-Six

After taking a day to recover, I headed to check on Pepper. She was still confused over exactly what had happened, but understood she would need to wait a while to get her answers. I tried my best to console her for the loss of the relationship she thought she'd been forming. The same applied to Vanessa, who learned of her newest boyfriend's fate when she returned from her cruise.

As a way to try to help the ladies move on, I offered both of them six months of free services at T.A.F.T.. They were both pleased with the offer and jumped at the chance.

The police had finally worked through the international red tape and were able to get the account information for Paul in the Caymans. After they had that, they were able to better investigate the evidence at each crime scene. Not only were they able to tie the account to Paul, they were able to tie it to his fingerprint specifically, which was on file with the bank.

Whether this happened because Paul and Kyle didn't know their fingerprints were different, it was an oversight on their part, or for some reason Paul did it intentionally, we didn't know. Paul was still not confessing to anything.

The initial trial where he would enter his plea was set for next month. As of now, it looked like he was steadfast in pleading guilty to attempted assault, but not guilty to all other charges. We'd just have to wait and see.

Now, it was back to the normal grind. Currently, I was headed to the grocery store. Jack had texted and asked me to pick up some milk and chocolate sauce.

My hopes fell when I got to the aisle that contained the chocolate sauce and found the shelf empty. Turning, I noticed a stock boy just down the aisle.

"Excuse me." I moved closer. "Can you check the back to see if you might have some more chocolate sauce? You're out."

The young man spun around and said, "Sure. I'll be right back."

As I waited, a familiar voice sounded from behind me. "Is this what you're looking for?"

I pivoted and ended up looking down. Behind me knelt Jack, holding a bottle of chocolate sauce. Slid onto its flip-top lid was a ring. My mouth fell open.

"Calla Lily Bloom. I have waited what feels like a lifetime to find the right woman. Not only are you the right woman for me personally, you accept that I have a dangerous job professionally and you jump in to help me to solve the unsolvable. You are the smartest, bravest, sexiest woman alive. I want nothing more than to have us spend the rest of our lives together. Will you marry me?"

The breath squeaked out of my lungs. Marry? As the words sunk in, my heart became overwhelmed with joy. I couldn't believe he'd brought me back to where it had all started with our very first kiss.

Even though emotionally I was thrilled, mentally I couldn't help but let a tickle of worry race down my spine as I thought about my previous marriage and subsequent divorce. Was I ready for this again? Could I risk getting hurt and hurting my family again?

I quickly ran the various worst-case scenarios through my brain and hesitated for the briefest of moments before I gazed down at Jack. The moment our gazes locked, all of the doubts vanished, and I knew I was ready, but only because he was the one asking and he was most definitely worth the risk.

"Yes. I will!" I launched myself into his arms and showered him with kisses.

Epilogue

We held our wedding in the late fall when the foliage was at its most colorful and the heat wasn't as intense. Gin had been kind enough to offer up her home—and the enormous grounds it was situated on—for our wedding.

The ceremony was small and consisted of only family and a few friends. We'd had enough limelight lately with the media attention the trial had gotten, not to mention Evelyn's YouTube video, which was still going strong.

Paul—in regard to the theft—had been found guilty of wire fraud and felony theft while taking. As far as the rest of the charges, he'd been convicted of attempted assault and accessory after the fact. Murder had been taken off the table when only his fingerprint had been found at the storage unit. All of the blood evidence had been tied to Kyle's DNA. With all the combined charges, Paul was looking at a minimum of twenty-plus years.

"I have one last surprise for you," Jack whispered after he finished sealing our I do's with a kiss.

"Yeah, what's that?"

Jack took my hand and pulled me along under a shower of rose petals thrown by our guests.

We reached the reception area. In the middle stood the most beautiful, unique cake I'd ever seen. It was shaped to impersonate a large bowl of ice cream covered with rich, dark chocolate sauce.

www.ingramcontent.com/pod-product-compliance
Lightning Source LLC
Chambersburg PA
CBHW031234120726
47905CB00002B/597